CW01590480

Aphrodite's Island

Aphrodite's Island

Andrew John Garcia

EFSTATHIADIS GROUP

EFSTATHIADIS GROUP S.A.
14, Valtetsiou Str.
106 80 Athens
Tel: (01) 5254650, 6450113
Fax: (01) 5254657
GREECE

ISBN 960 226 566 3

Printed and bound in Greece

for
EFTIHIA

Table of Contents

FOREWORD

This is a book of erotic stories. All the stories were written on a Greek island. I was in love, a love I had found while on holiday, the year before. It was summer, we lived on a quiet hillside in a tiny village. There was no television or other distraction. I had many hours to kill throughout three long summers, because my partner was running a shop on the island.

I had decided to write a textbook about my work. But try as I might I had no real heart for it. With the scent of the pines and the hillside herbs all around, with the sense of romance that comes with falling in love and having time to spare in a beautiful place, erotic thoughts kept intruding and formed themselves into stories. In order to get them out of my mind I noted them down. In the end I gave up the original project and the stories took over. They are all about encounters on an imaginary Greek island, Aphrodite's Island.

I wanted to write stories which in some way celebrated the joy of life and especially of our most secret sexual selves. I wanted to value each person's sexuality for what it is, no matter how perverse or unusual: ultimately it is a celebration not just of the goddess Aphrodite, but of life itself.

Enjoy.

Please note that while the stories originate from real experiences, some told to me, others observed, others again personal, all characters and places are fictional and do not in any way represent real persons or places.

Andrew John Garcia,
February 1998.

1. The Virgin

Liza couldn't believe her eyes. There hadn't been any seats left on the crowded ferry, so she and her three women travelling companions had found an empty spot and sat themselves down on the deck, spreading out their sleeping bags, and using their rucksacks as pillows to lean their heads on. This was to be a night crossing, and others around them had also been staking out their territory.

She had watched the people. There were Greek parents shepherding young children and talking loud and fast to each other, and other more peasant-looking people with simple clothes, wrinkled, dark skins and eyes full of a deep, natural wisdom. There had also been foreign tourists like herself, identifiable because of their fair, Northern skins. She had been particularly taken by the tall, beautiful, blond couple, who she'd assumed must be Swedish. The man had fine features, golden brown skin, and long golden hair tied back into a pony tail. The woman was his more feminine twin, with the same slim, angular beauty, long, thick golden hair and brown skin. Liza had felt fat, stunted and ugly by comparison.

She had turned away. From where she was, she could look down onto the dock. They'd been trying for some time, with loud curses, to load a large lorry which just wouldn't seem to get on board. They had just finally squeezed it in, when along the dock, with a roar of its engine, had come a large black motorcycle.

It was this that had so startled Liza. Driving it was a young woman who seemed to have confidently thrown convention to the winds. She was wearing shiny black leather, which beautifully complemented the shiny black of the bike - merely a waistcoat, long boots, gloves, and the briefest of leather briefs. Her limbs, most of which were exposed by this get-up, were tanned dark brown and shone with oil. Her black hair had been fashioned into spikes and stood like nails on the top of her head.

She seemed to look up for a moment in Liza's direction, and Liza thought the young woman might be looking at her. But then she realised she wasn't. The Swede had left his partner and was leaning over the rail. They studied each other for a few moments. Then Motorbike made a small sign of greeting with one hand, and, looking in his direction, Liza noticed he made a small sign back.

For some reason Liza felt herself blush. There had been a curious eroticism about this exchange - an acknowledgement of mutual admiration and desire.

Suddenly the young woman called something in Greek to a crew member within the bowels of the ship, the engine roared again, and the bike was up the ramp and gone. The Swede continued looking at the scene for a while, before returning to his partner, but Liza could see his attitude was now somehow different, more impatient, restless.

Two hours later, Liza was still wide awake. No matter what she did, sleep wouldn't come. The others had settled themselves down and were apparently sleeping without a problem. The ferry had eventually set off into the darkness, the bustle had subsided, and there were snores from all around. She decided to go looking for a coffee. She found the cafeteria, which was crowded, and stood at the bar. She tried to make herself understood but the barman refused to make the effort and kept serving others, Greeks, who barged in as if she wasn't there, or worse, actively pushed her out of the way.

Eventually a man whom she was somewhat in the way of, came to her rescue.

'You want a coffee?' She nodded. '*Nescafe metrio yia tyn copella sas parakalo.*' (A coffee please for the young woman).

She tried to thank the man but he had only wanted to buy his own coffee and he ignored her. She sat at a table next to the wall and sipped her drink.

After a while Motorbike arrived, and bought a beer. Liza noticed how easily she commanded instant attention at the bar, and even shouldered a man out of the way who tried to push in. People were looking at her, especially the men, but she took no notice, just sat down, lit a cigarette, and raised her bottle to her lips.

Again Liza felt inadequate. No one was looking at *her*.

Suddenly she realised a man had entered and was standing over the young woman. It was the big Swede. He greeted her. She smiled back, there was a pause. Then his hand went out and brutally stroked the spikes on her head. They flattened and sprung up again. Liza's throat went dry. She found herself longing for a beautiful man to want to do that to her. Would the young woman be angry? She ought to be. But she evidently wasn't. She simply looked at him. Neither spoke. Then she slowly and deliberately put out her cigarette, put the makings in her bag, drained her bottle, got up, and left. The Swede followed, just as casually, giving the room a contemptuous glance round as he went through the door.

Finishing her own drink, Liza gathered her things. Maybe she could find a dark place to sleep somewhere in the bowels of the ship rather than on deck. Perhaps that way she would avoid disturbing distractions like the encounter she had just witnessed. She took a stairway leading downwards. She came to a door - it didn't say you could go in, but it didn't say you couldn't since there was no notice on it at all. She went in. She found herself in a corridor with cabins along one side, and began walking down it. Turning a sudden corner she was confronted with a sight which took her breath away.

In front of her, in just the sort of space she was looking for, were Motorbike and the Swede. They were naked, and they were making love.

Virgin that she was, Liza stood there with her mouth gaping, frozen to the spot, watching the two bodies writhing together on the floor, and listening to the suppressed grunts and squelching noises they made.

Suddenly Motorbike's eyes widened, she let out a single shout, and Liza could see both bodies go still, then pulsate in waves of pleasure that seemed to go on and on, until finally they subsided, and the two of them collapsed in a sweaty heap.

They both stayed motionless for a few moments, gasping for air. Then suddenly Motorbike laughed, turning her eyes on Liza.

'*Diaskédases?*'

Liza didn't understand.

'You enjoy?'

Realising what she had done, she was covered in confusion.

'I'm sorry' she stuttered and quickly retraced her steps, not stopping till she was outside again leaning on the rail looking out, in the fresh night air, into the blackness.

She was still there hours later as the ferry docked. Liza aimlessly watched. Even in the calm, sunny weather of today she could see it was a tricky operation - the ferry had to turn itself round then accurately impale itself on the end of a thin stub of concrete that projected from the shore. A kind of mating. But very different from the scene she had witnessed the night before.

All night she had been struggling with a mass of thoughts. So far as she was concerned, and had been led to believe in the strictly religious country community where she was raised, life consisted of study and work. Eventually you fell in love and got married. You had children. Yes, there were pleasures - she enjoyed reading, the cinema, sports. But the idea of openly enjoying physical pleasure was entirely new to her, and both fascinating and shocking at the same time.

And now the possibility had presented itself to her, startlingly, incontrovertibly, in the form of two lovers, naked, copulating like two farm animals, in a public place. She wanted to be angry, but she couldn't.

As she pictured the scene again and again she began to feel herself erotically stirred, as if an inner energy had been contacted, that had somehow been dormant until now. She tried to think of other things, but her thoughts kept straying back.

Yes, she knew about physical pleasure in a way, but she had always seen it as an aside. Something that wasn't really important. This clear commitment to the body seemed alien, yet she found herself desperately wanting to partake of it.

She recognised the woman's short, stocky build combined with bodily strength, as similar to her own. Yet there was a confidence about this woman that Liza did not have. She remembered that, before the ferry left, she had been watching the activity on the dock-side and had seen her arrive on her motorbike. She had handled the powerful and heavy machine with ease and dominance, as if it were a well-trained slave expected to do its duty - and it did so. Liza, brought up on a farm, had driven first tractors and then her elder brothers' motorbikes herself, but had viewed her own facility with machines as an embarrassment, as if it somehow detracted from her sense of being female. Yet here was someone for whom it seemed to have the opposite effect - no less than turning her into a rampantly female, rampantly sexual being.

The powerful erotic effect was enhanced by how the woman presented herself with her shiny leather and spiked hair. It had never occurred to Liza that she could deliberately dress herself in a sexual way. Indeed this would be frowned on by both her parents and her friends, although for different reasons. Her parents would see it as social degradation to look anything other than respectably neutral sexually. As if, if you did anything else, you were joining those mysterious beings called prostitutes who sold themselves for she knew not what. Her friends, who were all committed to women's rights, would see it as selling out to men. It was taken for granted that you did nothing at all to attract men. In fact, many of them seemed to be deliberately repelling them.

Liza was reminded that her own shock of unruly fair hair was also closely cropped. Dorothy, the self-appointed leader of her party, had loudly announced the week before, in her usual bossy way:

"Crops all round lads."

Dorothy had this idea that they should all look the same - good for group identity and good for the heat. Liza thought it had more to do with Dorothy, who always did her best to look like a man and now was trying to get everyone else to do the same. She thought her hair, a rather styleless thatch admittedly, was OK as it was, and had resisted, but the others, and Dorothy herself, had gone off and got themselves short-back-and-sides at the men's hairdressers. They didn't look too bad, but not too good either, too butch for *her* taste. Then Dorothy had got bossy and two days ago had virtually ordered her to go and get it cut or she would do it herself one night when Liza was sleeping in her tent. It was said jokingly, but there was an edge to it, and knowing Dorothy, she thought she was quite capable of it.

Liza had angrily marched out, banging the door, and gone straight down to the barber's on the corner, and sat in line with the men. It was a cheap place, and the barber worked quickly, moving through the queue of about six in front of her in what seemed no time. In the chair, the cape round her, she'd grumpily told the completely unsurprised old barber that she wanted it as short as it could be and still have hair. Almost immediately, her head had been pushed roughly forwards and in a few strokes of the clipper the thatch was on the floor and had been replaced by a quarter-inch crop which made her look, she thought, like a mass murderer just released from prison.

Now, on the ferry, she touched it and found that it did have something. It was sort of soft and bristly at the same time. But would a man want to stroke it, as Motorbike had had hers stroked? She wasn't sure.

And then there was the idea of sex. This young woman obviously attracted men and had attracted the young man, even though he was clearly a stranger and with a partner. To have sex so casually was totally repulsive, irresponsible and immoral behaviour in Liza's eyes, yet it strangely interested her as much as it repelled her. But would he want to do that to her? She felt in no danger, and was disappointed.

She didn't see herself as attractive. Here she was at nineteen, a whole year at university and still did not have a boy friend, let alone a lover, like so many other girls she knew.

Up till now this hadn't really bothered her too much - she had always assumed, with her parents' encouragement, that it would happen in its own good time. She had her exams to pass, she had lots of interests and friends. There was plenty to fill her life. Yet she was still aware that the boys at school and now at university seemed to look through her - it was as if she wasn't there.

It was a mystery to her why this might be. After all, she was always neat, clean, and well turned out. There was nothing frighteningly ugly about her features, they were a bit pugnacious, that's all. But she liked her large, deep blue eyes, and her skin, which was naturally smooth, almost hairless. Her complexion was perfect and she neither wore nor possessed makeup. And although she never displayed them, even hid them under loose clothing whenever possible, she was proud of her large, perfectly-formed breasts.

She'd joined the women's group at the start of the first term of her economics course. There she found that the women liked her, and she liked them. When she'd tentatively mentioned her experience with boys, Dorothy, who was leader of that group, had explained to her.

'Men are all the same - looking for stereotyped beauty - sex objects to wank over in bed at night.'

It needed some special man to appreciate her qualities. Perhaps, she had allowed herself to imagine when she had decided to go on this holiday, a Greek, who would see her for the beauty she was and sweep her off her feet.

But the truth was, there was no real chance of that - she just wasn't attractive enough and there was bound to be plenty more young women from which to choose. She decided she would concentrate on the camping and walking and forget about romance for the duration.

'Hi. Couldn't you sleep?'

It was her three travelling companions. Dorothy put her arm round her and gave her a friendly hug.

'Where are we?'

'An island. Come on, we're getting off: it's an opportunity. The ferry hardly ever stops here - it's only doing it now because of the good weather.'

Hurriedly collecting her things, and rather reluctant at this apparently cavalier change of plan, Liza followed her companions off the boat.

Arriving on the quayside, she paused to adjust her high backpack to make it more comfortable. As she did so, she was aware of a pair of eyes staring at her.

They came from where a knot of people were waiting, watching the arrival.

They belonged to a man standing perhaps ten metres away, who was dressed very simply in denim shorts and a T-shirt, seemed to be in his thirties, had short, thick, greying hair and was very tanned. He was handsome, she thought. They were brown, the eyes, bright, intelligent, and piercing. There was no criticism in the look at all, just frank, warm admiration.

'Liza. Here.'

Dorothy had realised she had lagged behind and was calling her. She moved towards a very old looking bus, which stood behind the knot of people. To do this, however, she found that she had to push past the man, and as their bodies touched, there was a brief, intense eye-contact again. He seemed on the verge of speaking, but she was embarrassed and walked on.

Her rucksack was promptly removed from her and dumped into an enormous boot, already full with cases. She just had time to see the lid tied down with a flimsy piece of string before she was bundled impatiently into the interior.

She found herself crushed in next to a Greek woman in black, with an enormous handbag, and an assortment of other locals all talking loudly. As the bus pulled away she could see the man kissing a young woman goodbye before walking over to a dusty red Landrover and getting in. There was something about the kiss which indicated that perhaps it was his daughter.

Settling back in her seat, as the bus started and began to jolt its way along the rough road towards the town and eventually, she assumed, the campsite, she felt confused and surprised. Also a little excited and pleased. And intrigued. She had definitely been looked at admiringly - there was no mistaking the expression on the man's face or the look in his eyes - dare she say it - he had desired her.

Maybe he had seen her breasts. Perhaps she could discreetly begin to make a bit more of them. She let herself fantasise a little. He wanted to fondle them and to caress and erect the nipples, and lift them, feeling their glorious weight. Kiss them... She stopped herself. Someday a man *would* want to do this to her, but she could feel herself responding sexually so she decided to concentrate on the surrounding countryside. This seemed to be rocky and parched. Most unappealing. There was also the strange and terrifying din of what must be cicadas. She had read about them. She wanted desperately to go home.

As the bus moved on through the island, there were various changes of passengers, parcels were taken on board, the driver even stopped for coffee at a tiny wayside bar, sitting and chatting with the owner for what seemed like ages. They waited in silence, in the broiling heat, until the driver deigned to continue the journey with neither explanation nor apology.

Dorothy had seemed unconcerned - she was busy studying the map, and reading the guidebook.

Suddenly, the bus was traversing a delightful town square shaded by huge palms and strange trees with enormous red flowers on them. Almost toppling into their path were street cafes at which indolent-seeming people, most of them looking unbelievably beautiful to Liza's untrained English eye, were sipping drinks. This was quickly lost from sight as the bus turned a corner and plunged down the narrowest of main streets, dived under an ancient arch, and emerged a moment later to be, it seemed, suspended in space.

To their right were the imposing walls of an ancient castle, to their left, nothing - just air, with, way below them, the most amazing sight she had ever seen. It was a semi-circular bay with a tiny beach complete with tiny people sitting on it, tiny white houses, a tiny forest of trees behind it, and tiny boats anchored in brilliant Mediterranean-blue water. She could see every detail.

To her amazement, the bus didn't pause for a moment. Instead, the driver seemed determined to kill them all. Swearing at other drivers and occasional pedestrians, he sped down a snaking narrow road that descended the edge of the cliff on which, clearly, the town and castle were built. There was no such thing as a safety barrier. By the time they had descended and screeched to a halt at the bottom under pine trees, Liza's hands were wet with sweat.

Dorothy hadn't apparently noticed their danger.

'Come on, slow coach, off'.

Liza realised that it was the end of the line, and they were the last passengers left on board. They found themselves deposited, with their bags, at the entrance to the campsite.

With the experiences of the previous day running round in her head all night, Liza found it next to impossible to wake up next morning to Dorothy's urgent shakes and warnings.

She had a slight headache and asked to be excused that day's walking. She drifted back to sleep, while the others went off in a bright, chattering bunch. It was mid morning before she emerged from her tent, hardly aware of where she was - all she knew was that they'd pitched their tents, spent a lazy day on the beach, grabbed something to eat, and gone to bed early. But it was invigorating to find herself in a pleasantly shady grove of trees with the scent of pines in her nostrils and the cheerful call of cicadas all around. Having freshened up, she was just about ready to begin thinking about breakfast, when she saw, with a little shock, about a hundred yards away, to the right, beyond some slender trees, the dusty old Landrover from the day before.

Curious, she approached it, moving from tree to tree. There he was, with his back to her, sitting at a small table in the shade next to the camp site bar. He had a long drink in front of him and was sipping it. He was alone and there were only one or two other people in the bar area.

She hesitated. What she was contemplating was the action of a brazen hussy, a harlot and a trollop. These were words she had heard used in her village with the utmost condemnation of young women who pushed themselves forward too much where men were concerned. But there was a stronger force acting, and it had to do with the heat of the sun, and the scent of the pines, and the call of the cicadas, and it came from deep inside her. If Motorbike could do it, so could she.

She started walking as nonchalantly as she could towards the bar. The nearer she got, the more nervous she became, and she had to force herself to go on. She began unbuttoning her shirt as she walked, her hands seeming to work by themselves, baring a strip of skin right down to her waist with more than a hint of breast. Yes she was a brazen hussy, no doubt about it.

Getting to the bar, her voice somehow got stuck in her throat, but she managed to ask for a yogurt and a coffee.

Now she had to do it just right. Keeping her eyes firmly lowered, as if she needed to do this to avoid spilling her drink, she advanced towards the tables, selecting one right in front of him.

She sat down and began spooning yogurt into her mouth, as if deep in thought.

Well, the yogurt eventually came to an end, and the coffee. As casually as she could, she leaned back in her chair and raised her eyes.

She found she was now fully engaging this other pair of eyes - they were warm, intense, unflinching, admiring, exactly as before.

She found herself smiling.

'Hi,' he said. 'Where are you from?' It was excellent English with only the slightest Greek accent.

They started going through the pleasantries. He didn't try to force himself on her - just showed interest, that was all. She discovered his name was Petros and that he was a lecturer at an English university, in art history. He stayed here, where he had built a house, for most of the summer. The idea was to get on with his own painting, rather than talking about other people's, as he did for the rest of the year, but it never quite happened. He was a bit of a recluse and was divorced. He had a teenage daughter who he had been seeing off at the harbour yesterday, after a fortnight's stay.

So far as she was concerned, he'd guessed most of it, from what he'd seen on the quayside - the four girls, the walking holiday, even about Dorothy and her sexuality.

'She's gay,' he said emphatically.

'She may be but I'm not,' she replied a little too heatedly.

His eyes focused firmly on her again.

Suddenly he was moving. 'I was on my way to the beach - just called in for a drink.' Then, with studied casualness:

'I can give you a lift to the beach if you like.'

She was being picked up. She was amazed. Liza, who everyone ignored, had been singled out. She flushed. But there was no doubt about it. She was indeed being picked up. It was important not to panic. She must stay calm. But part of her was rebelling. She should refuse. She didn't know this man. He might want sex with her. But then, she wanted sex with him, didn't she? That's why she was there. In a sense he hadn't picked her up at all. She'd done it to him. She'd seen him sitting there and done it, just like Motorbike. True, he wasn't the beautiful Swede. Actually, she wasn't at all sure she'd be interested if it was. No, this one was much more to her taste. She realised she was hesitating, and if she did it for too long she would lose the opportunity she had created.

Then she realised that she was committing herself to nothing at all if she accepted. It was only the beach. She could tag along, see where it went, make choices on the way. Play with him a bit. Tantalise him. She liked this idea. Life was looking up. Yes, she did want to continue it.

'OK. I'd love to.'

Excitedly, she returned quickly to her little igloo tent and was naked in a trice. Then she fished in her rucksack for her swimsuit, and when she took it out, realised with dismay that it was a frilly, ill-conceived nonsense, bought when she was still at school, and highly inappropriate for an experienced young woman. Fortunately, as she'd pulled out the swimsuit, her tanga had also fallen out.

The tanga was the briefest imaginable of swimsuits. Simply a tiny triangle at the front, to cover the pubes, two thongs which went over the hips, and another thong at the back which went between the cheeks of the backside, leaving them completely exposed to public view. There was no top to a tanga - it was assumed you would naturally want to be topless.

It had been Dorothy's idea again. She wanted them, as a group, to all put them on together in order to shock the other tourists on the beach. At one of the planning sessions between the four of them, which weren't really planning sessions at all, because they consisted of Dorothy announcing what she had in mind for all of them, she had produced these articles and thrust one at each of them. Although she'd packed it, Liza had actually forgotten about it, and had not even tried it on. Now, lying there on the floor of the tent, it seemed just the thing. She was very happy to go topless, even though it was going to be her first time, because this way he could get a full view of her lovely breasts. And wearing the tanga was no problem either because then he could see how tight and muscular her backside and thighs were.

Impulsively, she slipped it on. She was delighted with how tightly and briefly the triangle gripped her pubis, showing on either side just a little hair. Since she was blonde it didn't really show, so she was satisfied proper decency was observed. She snapped the side thongs onto her thighs and wriggled slightly to ease the back thong into its crease. This was pleasurable too, because it also suddenly snapped into place against her anus, sending a little thrill from it up into the rest of her body, and then continued to apply a slight pressure which she was subtly aware of as she moved.

Then she was back into her shorts and shirt, and, with her towel and sun cream, heading back to the bar.

The short ride to the beach in Petros's car was inconsequential. Once on the beach, he started putting down his beach mat, and organising his stuff. Inspired by the glorious sun, and the inviting crystal clear water, the most incredible green colour, she threw caution to the winds, pulled off her shirt and shorts, plunged into the refreshing liquid, swam out far into the middle of the bay, then wallowed lazily for a while.

Then she remembered Petros, and approached the shore. There he was, watching her return. She flopped down on her back beside him, totally unselfconscious now, and spread her legs, so as to allow herself to dry in the sun.

This was the moment when she was half expecting him to make a move - ruffle her crewcut, perhaps - she was longing for him to do that - others had ruffled it, she knew what that felt like, very friendly, but to have it ruffled in passion, well, that would be very special. But nothing happened. After a few minutes she heard him speaking.

'Mm?'

'You ought to put some cream on,' he repeated.

She was longing to ask him to do it for her, but she was afraid she was already appearing too brazen. So instead she sat up and slopped some on her front, then remembering his presence, taking special care of her breasts, massaging them and getting them to poke out a bit more. Then stopping herself again because she didn't want to overdo it and look like a hussy. She turned over and took the risk then of offering him the bottle.

He did her back, a little tentatively at first, but then more confidently, his hands clearly quite skilful. It was her first taste of being massaged by a man and she enjoyed it, surrendering easily to the feel of the strong hands, giving him little "mm's" of pleasure to encourage him to go on. His hands worked down her back.

'How about the *poppó* - the bottom?' he asked.

‘Please,’ she said as casually as she could.

And then she could feel the cheeks of her backside being unceremoniously done over, before moving on to do the backs of her thighs and legs. It was so good, and when he had finished, she longed to ask him to do it all again, but was afraid to do so.

Then they lay on their fronts in the sun talking easily of all sorts of matters from the importance of putting on plenty of sun block to walking holidays and the colour of grass in England as opposed to Greece, and would the two countries be indistinguishable if they had the same weather.

He looked at his watch. It was lunchtime, and would she like a Greek salad and wine at the villa, an invitation she accepted with alacrity.

Two hours later they were finishing their meal, sitting on his terrace in the shade of a vine thick with ripening grapes, and looking out from high up over the village, its white cubes of houses tumbling away beneath them, down to the blue waters of the bay and the sea beyond.

With disappointment she realised that, although he clearly desired her, he still hadn’t made a proper sexual move - he’d been circling round it, playing with the idea, trying to decide. It would be very easy for this to turn into a very nice friendship, with nothing else spoken between them. This was not what she wanted. Once again, she had to act. Now was the opportunity because there was a lull in the conversation, and they were just sitting there gazing out to sea, saying nothing.

Once again, some inner compulsion overcame her doubts and with a certainty that surprised her she stood up, went round to his side of the table, leant over him, put her arms round his shoulders and laid her cheek on his head. His hair was soft.

After a few moments like this he stood up and opened his arms for her. She entered them and allowed him to hold her tight for a while. She felt very secure there.

For a moment she was stuck. She hadn't yet ever kissed in a sexual way - she didn't know what to do. She would have to simply follow his lead, do what he did, but how to get him leading?

Then she took an image from an old black and white film she'd seen. She closed her eyes firmly, raised her lips, pouting them slightly, put one hand on the back of his neck - she had to stretch up, it seemed, a long way to do it - and firmly but gently pulled his head down. Finally his lips brushed hers.

Then she felt them move on their own at last, and gently do it again. They got into a long sequence of these gentle kisses. Then his mouth opened and he was suddenly kissing her more forcefully, kneading his mouth against hers. Then he began using his tongue, flicking it in and out of her mouth.

She was surprised at first. She didn't know what to do. It felt very odd having a mouth thrust at you all wet and slobbering like this. Her first instinct was to pull away and say 'nasty', like you would to a child, but then she realised this must be sex and if she let go and allowed it to happen she might actually enjoy it, and to her surprise this is exactly what happened. More than that, there was something exciting about it and she wanted more of it and to do it to him, so she did - she repeated the action and this seemed to drive him on. And she was getting driven on, too, enjoying the wetness and the exciting feelings that came with it.

Then she felt his tongue go hard and stiff, like a little penis, and be forced deep into her mouth - signal of his intention. She knew what to do. She didn't know how, but she did. She sucked on it, used her own tongue on it, to show her own intention, and then he had pulled apart and was gently leading her into the house and into the bedroom.

It was cool in there, with a smooth tiled floor and cane furniture. There was a large double bed.

Her knees went weak, and she began to shake uncontrollably. He must have interpreted this as passion, rather than fear resulting from simple inexperience, and while she shook, he unbuttoned her shirt, and slid it off. Then he took her breasts in his hands to fully appreciate them, caressing them first, then bending to kiss them and flick the nipples erect with his tongue. This excited her so much she pulled his head back up to her face for a moment's respite. She didn't know she could respond so easily. She was shocked at herself. But she loved it, loved it - and found herself whispering it to him over and over.

Then he was kissing her again, using his mouth and tongue circling wider and wider - cheeks, eyes, forehead, hair, then down the neck, onto the breasts, sucking them again, mercilessly, and giving little bites to the nipples.

Now she surrendered utterly to the sensations - different ones coming thick and fast, so the shaking was now no longer of fear, but simply of utter ecstasy.

Finally he was sliding his tongue down to her navel and was on his knees before her. Deftly he unhooked the stud at the top of her shorts, letting them drop. She was still wearing the tanga. This he unceremoniously took by the sides and pulled downwards, so it hung in a very undignified manner half way down her legs.

Her bush of fair pubic hair was exposed now, and she smiled to see him bury his face in it to get the smell of it, and stroked the top of his head, then gave a short cry, taking bunches of his hair, as she felt his tongue, this searching tongue of his, flick open the lips of her vagina and probe into it again and again, which she could feel instantly irrigating and responding, and then searching upwards and locking firmly onto her clitoris.

She was clutching and scratching at his head now, as pre-orgasmic waves began to pulse round her body.

Clearly realising this, and in his own urgency, he desisted from what he was doing, and pressed her gently backwards onto the bed. She opened her legs....

And then suddenly she realised there was a hitch. He'd gone. She could hear him next door, in what must be the bathroom, desperately opening and closing cupboards, and then knocking over tins and jars until finally reappearing, naked and triumphant, his erection sticking ludicrously upwards in front of him, holding up - what was it?

A packet of condoms! Condoms! She'd forgotten about condoms! So convinced of her own ugliness, of the lack of interest of men in her, of the unlikeliness of *anything happening* had she been, that she hadn't bothered to buy any.

She felt a warm glow towards him, holding out her arms and smiling as he got onto the bed between her splayed legs, condom now hurriedly rolled into place. Using one hand to guide the glans of his penis to the opening, he slid it smoothly in, right up to the hilt, and then lowered himself until he was heavy on top of her, and was still for a moment.

Now she discovered how delightful it was to have the weight of a man on her. Her body felt strong, and perfectly capable of supporting it, with ease and comfort.

She was also surprised that her vagina had not resisted in any way. It was ready, it was oiled, and it received. She thought it was supposed to be painful the first time - blood on the sheets and all that - but clearly not for her.

And she could feel the penis inside her. Once it was in, her vagina had known exactly what to do, and had somehow locked itself around its guest, holding and enveloping it. And there was a delicious feeling of penetration - she could feel the end of the penis gently knocking on the end wall of the vagina deep inside as he made tiny movements.

Then he had raised himself slightly and was looking into her eyes. He began to move in and out. Closing her eyes and concentrating on maximising the good feelings, she found that by pushing upwards herself, she could engage her clitoris on its way up with the root of his penis coming down. Together with the wonderful feelings issuing from inside the vagina this gave an added pulse of pleasure.

Now he was kissing her, tonguing her, and she was doing the same back, and then both kneading and stroking, everywhere they could find. Their movements became more violent, their pubes slamming into each other at the end of each stroke, until, very suddenly, with a cry, she knew her orgasm was on her, but so did he, because he cried out too, and they both exploded with gasps and spasms, finally collapsing, he again onto her, and lay still for a long time, panting, recovering.

Now she felt peaceful, warm. She stroked his head gently as he lay there. He was hers. There was a sense in which she owned him a little bit now.

His penis was still inside her, and she could feel it getting smaller and smaller until it finally, almost on its own, popped out, a bit like a cork from a bottle.

He sat up a bit and pulled the condom off - the penis underneath now looking wet and soggy - very sorry for itself indeed. He tied a quick knot in the end of the condom and chucked it towards a bin on the other side of the room - he missed by a long way.

He looked at her, doubt in his eyes.

'A bit brief, I'm afraid.'

'Short but very sweet.' She wanted to reassure, and she was being honest - it had been alot better than the inadequate, fumbling first experiences she'd heard described by friends and acquaintances.

'I was desperate,' he said. 'I wanted you so much.'

'I wanted *you* so much,' she said.

They smiled again at each other, then lay and slept for an hour before she left him to take a shower. When she returned to the room, he went for a shower too.

There was a full length mirror on one wall of the room, and she went over to it.

She'd been standing in front of the mirror for she didn't know how long, admiring herself, in her full naked simplicity, and coping with the idea that she was now not looking at a virgin but a slut. She repeated it to herself, over and over. A slut, pure and simple. An utter slut, a brazen hussy, a harlot and a trollop. The words produced a strange mixture of feelings inside. Wanting to be like Motorbike was one thing. But actually doing it was another.

Then she realised he'd been watching her and had come up close behind her. He too was admiring her in the mirror. Then he put both arms around her from behind, and they looked together at the effect - a couple. A beautiful couple. And yes, she was beautiful, not in the standard way peddled by cosmetics adverts, cold and aloof, but in her own way, with directness and warmth. And she was feminine, and not in a sentimental, soft way but in a muscular, strong way. And her short hair, far from detracting from the effect, added to it, pale gold at the sides where it lay close to her head, and a richer, darker gold on top, where its strong spines stood erect. Now she could see exactly why he had picked her out.

He had clearly seen her eyes flick up, because now he started running his hand through her hair, not in a friendly way at all, but with intention and, yes, with passion, enjoying the blonde spikes, as they flicked up and down beneath his hand, just as she had wanted on the beach. The effect on her was electric. Her body glowed and she began moving her head, to help him, and to show her pleasure, and closed her eyes, surrendering to the sensation.

Then he wrapped his arms round her to hold and squeeze her breasts, and nuzzling her head forward, he was able to bite and suck on the exposed nape of her neck. It too was a delicious sensation, and she could feel his penis forming hard against the small of her back....

Then she had her eyes open. He had whispered a request in her ear 'Let me...'

With a little look of surprised innocence, fear and questioning, she pulled a little away.

He responded, not by stopping, but by biting her ear gently, and whispering the request again.

Then she smiled, archly, and found herself answering him by twisting her head round, kissing him fully and lingeringly on the mouth, and then thrusting her tongue deep and hard into the cavity. Yes, she wanted it. She wanted all he had to offer.

When she got back to the site, not too late as she didn't want the others to be worried about her, she found they had returned, had had their showers, and were now contemplating food.

They were so excited by their own experiences involving a visit to a ruined castle deep in the interior of the island, that they barely noticed her. Had they or had they not seen, or at least felt, the souls of the dead out there in the strange, dusty heat? And, more importantly, what about the plight of the women, innocent pawns and chattels in all of this?

She was silent all evening. The joy she had experienced with Petros was somehow slipping away, leaving behind a dark, empty feeling. She felt sore now, and those words that had at first made her hesitate, kept echoing insistently in her head: brazen hussy, slut, harlot, trollop.

'What's wrong with you?'

It was Dorothy, and the voice was harsh and demanding.

She managed to stumble out something about meeting a man and making love. Then suddenly she was enveloped in a huge torrent of emotion that came from nowhere and had her floundering. She started to sob, deep, heartfelt sobs that wracked her body - grief, perhaps, for her lost innocence. And the truth was out - blurted, brutally, through the tears and sobs, the horrible truth.

'I'm a slut, harlot, and trollop. First I let him fuck me and then I let him do it again - twice. And in different ways. Sorry.'

There was stunned silence.

Then there were two big arms around her, some 'there there' noises and caresses, Dorothy actually attempting to be maternal, and she had been gently kissed on the cheek, released, and there was a good-hearted belly-laugh.

She found herself laughing, too - sobbing and laughing at the same time.

'Good for you. Good for you. I think this deserves champagne.'

2. The Demon Lover

Fucked once a month. That's how Connie saw it. Together eighteen years, two children that had come along almost immediately, the house - work, the effort of bringing them up, of making money, of advancing Michael's career, and now what?

Fucked once a month.

She looked at him sitting at the table opposite. He didn't seem to notice if she was there any more. Drinking his coffee, looking out to sea, looking at a pair of legs in a miniskirt going by, not one look at her.

And yet she was there, very there.

She knew that she was still a beautiful woman, even at 38, nearly 39. She had a statuesque, fine physique, which she kept in trim with daily workouts, long lonely walks, and swimming with the kids. And that brilliant, naturally blonde hair, it had been the thing that had made her the big catch. Abroad, people always thought she was Swedish, and then didn't believe it when she said she was English:

'Yes, but you must have Swedish blood.'

The blonde hair she could sit on. As a young girl it had shone so brightly. It was like a beacon for attracting men, some of them handsome, some rich, some clever, some all of those things. How it had turned them on!

And of all of them she had chosen Michael. Why? Well, to begin with he was beautiful, too. His own hair was naturally blonde, worn long, also, in a trendy pony tail. Women idolised him and Connie was no exception. And they looked so good together. So they had tried it out. She had been doubtful, and so had he. He liked brunettes really, he once confessed. And she didn't want a handsome layabout she would have to serve all her life. But he offered social acceptability, safety and dependability. And, for all his attractiveness to women, he was surprisingly innocent. As if all those past encounters had barely touched him. His innocence had seemed another attraction. She'd laughed over it with her girl friends. It had made him into a sweet, endearing little doll. But with this innocence of his had also come a self-absorption, an unawareness of her beauty, her needs. Now it seemed unbecoming. A real man would be able to court her and value her.

He'd come home, eaten his dinner, watched TV, gone to bed, and snored as usual for so many years now. He was too tired to make love to her because he fucked the secretaries at work, more than likely. All those late 'business conferences'. But she'd preferred not to ask any questions for the sake of the children. And what did he get enthusiastic about? Sailing. Damned sailing. And for all those years she'd accepted this as normal. As happiness. Their large house. The lovely garden. Dinners for work colleagues. Dinners for other couples. Petty rivalries with the neighbours over this and that. Buying the car. Buying the boat. All things *he* wanted, really. She had gone along with it. None of it hers. None of it what *she* wanted.

She was bored, she'd realised. She wanted more.

First it had been classes. Japanese flower arranging. Cake decoration. Then she'd joined an amateur dramatics group. There she'd been desired, flirted with. She'd liked it. She'd realised that yes, she still was beautiful. There had been a man, himself married, who'd gently propositioned her. It was a shock, but flattering. It had never occurred to her that she could, if she wanted, take a lover. And she was tempted. This shocked her even more. Of course, she was aware that other women took lovers. The cake decoration class had been a particularly sociable group, and after it was over they had taken to going to each others' houses for tea. Inevitably, among the other subjects that came up, the failings of their various partners had become a standing joke. A kind of group fantasy built up about the 'ideal man' who could not only mend a washing machine, but be sensitive to their needs and make powerful love on demand.

Among great laughter, it seemed that every woman in the room had a partner that failed, particularly in the latter department. Then Pat, a pretty mother of two, had announced that she had solved the problem.

'I have a lover,' she said.

They had all gone silent, desperate for more information, but hesitant to ask. All she would say was that he was

'A demon at making love - of course, he's Greek. Very passionate. Satisfies me completely.'

Desperate as they were to know more, they were all highly embarrassed at this direct mention of sexual passion and the talk had hurriedly gone onto other things. But occasionally, as the weeks passed, someone would ask 'How is the demon lover, Pat?' and get a 'Fine, thanks,' and a secretive smile in return.

A demon lover. Connie began to apply the possibility to herself. A demon lover, one that appeared when required, performed, and disappeared, suddenly seemed an attractive idea. She needed more passion in her life, that's what it was.

But taking a lover would be a defeat, in a way. Maybe Michael could still satisfy her. If only they could be on their own together away from the children and the distractions of running a home, things would happen. Then she hit on the idea of a foreign holiday - just the two of them. Let the kids, teenagers now, look after themselves, wreck the place with parties if they wanted, just so she and Michael could be alone. In his laid back way, he'd gone along with the idea. She'd found a fancy brochure offering away-from-it-all holidays on obscure Greek islands. She'd booked the whole thing. She'd packed for him. She'd got him to the airport. She'd even done a crash course in Greek and was very clear on the difference between *kalimera* and *kalispera*, and when not to use *kalinichta*.

But it hadn't worked, she'd known that from day one - he was still just as self-absorbed. She was a convenience, she realised, like his newspaper, like his boat.

She found after a couple of days' settling in, that she had an inner restless energy, a need, a desire, a new sense of her sexuality. Perhaps a first sense. Before, sex had been pushed to the sidelines. Now, in moments of boredom like the present one, fantasies had begun to emerge, as if by themselves, and the focus was the demon lover, as yet without a face. A man who could really satisfy her. Young. Dark. Sensitive. A man who knew about women. Would seduce her, very gently yet forcibly. Take her on mysterious, outrageous sexual adventures. Give her orgasm after orgasm. Since this image didn't fit any of the men she knew, she had made him foreign: Greek, like Pat's lover. A Greek man, simple in his tastes, but with a deep understanding and highly sexed. A man who, in the urgency of his need, would take her in all sorts of places. And of course she always had no choice. Though what happened was not strictly rape, somehow she knew she had to submit. And sometimes what she had to submit herself to shocked her in its outrageousness: Her dress being torn off, her underclothes cut to shreds, her bedcovers being ripped away. This ripping away was always important and strangely excited her.

And here on this island there were prospective demon lovers all around her - real Greek men, many of them so beautiful, so young, who seemed to possess just the qualities she had imagined. She began to feel sexual all the time. She loved the way they flaunted themselves on the streets. And the Greek men liked her, she could sense that. As she walked about the little town she could sense their eyes on her, their desire. And it thrilled her. She felt she grew a little taller under their gaze, a little more beautiful, a little more statuesque.

And it was still there, the hair, still the old beacon, just as strong, just as yellow. There had been a period when she had worn it a shorter, more sensible length, but over the last couple of years she had allowed it to grow again, though held discreetly up. Now, although she couldn't yet sit on it, she was aware that it would ride neatly across the small of her back as she walked, if she were to allow it to. And here, in Greece, she began to allow it to. And as she walked she let it swing, just as it had swung in the old days, and as she sat she flicked it, just as she had in the old days, and just as she had in the old days she put her hand in it and absently pulled it out so they could see its fullness and strength, and above all how long it was.

Reflecting on this, she became aware that an old, wrinkled fisherman was looking at her. He had an appreciative smile on his face. She was amused and pleased. She flicked and swung her hair for him, pulled it out with both her hands and let it drop, so he could admire it. Then she looked up and caught his eye, he winked and they both exchanged a laugh.

Michael looked grumpily up from yesterday's Telegraph.

'What are you laughing at?'

'Just an old man.'

But she was also aware that another pair of eyes were looking at her, young, dark, passionate. And they belonged to the young waiter, Stavros. There was an intensity about his look which excited her. He was talking now to a friend of his, but always his glance would creep in her direction. He was clearly undressing her, could see the delicate slimness of her waist, the rich womanliness of her hips, the proud fulness of her breasts. Suppose he were to come over, ask for a light, perhaps. No, better still, she would go inside seeking the toilet. There would be no one inside because at this season everyone was sitting outside under the umbrellas. Suddenly he would be there barring the way. She would ignore him, and try to push past, but he wouldn't let her. She would be forced to take notice of him and demand to be let by. Instead, he would catch her roughly by the shoulders and forcibly kiss her on the mouth. She would resist at first but quickly her passion would take over and she would kiss back, pulling him to her even more forcibly. Then she would be pushed back, there would be a fierce look in his eyes, her blouse would be grabbed and his two strong hands would rip it open at the front. The breasts would leap out...

'Let's move then, darling.'

'What?'

'Let's move. Take a stroll along the quay. See what shipping's come in over night.'

'I hope you don't mind, dear, but I'd quite like to walk up to the old town to look in the shops.'

A relieved expression came over Michael's face. It meant he could stand around and chat with the yachting types and the fishermen.

Later, as she slowly walked up the winding road towards the ancient stones of the castle, the sun beating down on her and the cicadas loud in her ears, she carried on with the fantasy. Stavros with his youthful, twinkling eyes, his dark skin and curly black hair, kept so short and neat, his clothes, too, just a cut-back T shirt and tiny shorts, always so clean, always carelessly exposing his muscles and health. His eyes especially would flick to the hair, then to the breasts, then to the legs, assessing all the time, assessing and lusting. And she loved it.

She would be pushed into the toilet, the door locked and there taken powerfully, simply, not because she was a person, but because she was female, and beautiful and on heat. And she was, she suddenly realised, desperately on heat. Taken from the rear, as she supported herself as best she could on the pipework around the cistern, his huge, hard cock ramming home again and again while she stifled her screams as best she could.

Stavros! Oh, Stavros! Stavros served at the taverna they had got into visiting most evenings - Michael loved habits. The place was quiet and it was by the sea, so he could inspect the yachts in the harbour. The food, while very Greek, was not too oily. And Stavros spoke a primitive form of English that delighted her over and over. Right from the first night he had spotted them, invited them in, showed them the kitchen, what was cooking, recommended what to have.

And she had found herself watching Stavros and slowly, as the days passed, becoming aware that he was watching her. When they arrived there would always be something special.

'Today you must try the goat in lemon sauce. It is truly exquisite...'

Then one day, about a week after their arrival, the looks changed to touches, secret ones. The meal finished, Stavros had brought brandy 'on the house, just for you, my special English friends'.

And they had talked about Buckingham Palace, the

Tower of London, all the tourist sights that Stavros might like to see if ever he left the island and came to England.

And as they were talking, Michael on one side of her and Stavros on the other, she felt, with a little thrill, Stavros getting closer and closer until his whole body seemed to be touching her. Then, outrageously, Stavros's hand had crept across her buttocks and then, because she gave no sign, got bolder, plunged into the long, golden tresses to stroke them, ever so gently at first, but much stronger later, as the evening wore on. And the conversation moved on as the evening did, both of them talking with Michael and other Greeks who drifted in, about this and that, especially boats and fishing, which fascinated Michael.

'And there was the time I caught a Moray eel. This thing can kill you in an instant, and there it was in the bottom of the boat about to attack me. So I made a dive, grabbed my knife, and as it struck, I cut its head off and do you know it still bit me - the head on its own bit me, and I have the scar to this day...'

And Michael countered with his own experiences of the cold English seas, quickly taking on the guise of an old salt, rather than the summer weekend sailor he really was.

All this with pantomimes and broken English and additions and verifications from others. And much laughter and much booze.

And she could see how Michael worshipped these men with their simple life, their adventures and knowledge of the sea, and longed to be respected by them.

And the hand got bolder all the time, and neither of them gave the slightest sign.

Passing finally under the battered old archway which once served as the outer defence against invaders, but now simply looked quaintly attractive, she wandered along the narrow cobbled main street, looking into what were once tiny houses but were now equally tiny shops.

She vaguely hoped Stavros would have seen where she was going and would have followed her. A hand would emerge from an alleyway, she would be pulled in, hot lips would be pressed against hers, while the clothes were torn off her, rip, rip, and gloriously naked, she would be raised high in the air and lowered onto the waiting phallus, full of its urgent juices...

Going into a shop she was welcomed by a young woman, very Greek and dark looking, with spiky black hair, a series of rings in one ear, and a bright, welcoming smile. Connie was stunned by what she wore.

'What are you looking at?'

'The dress.'

The young woman laughed, and did a twirl. It was a long, sleeveless dress, pure white, cut very slim and hugging to the body until just below the hips where it flared out down to the calves. But what was so stunning about it was the material from which it was made - a cotton woven so thin that below it the contours of the body could be seen, discreetly yet perfectly. She could see the young woman's ample breasts and dark nipples, the hint of the groove of her backside as she twirled, and most shocking of all, the triangular outline of her pubic hair at her crotch.

'I have one in your size - would you like to try it on?'

She demurred.

'Oh, no. I'm too old for such a thing. It's OK for young people like you.'

'Young? How old do you think I am? I'm 38, you know.'

She was confounded. The 'young' woman was the same age as herself. Suddenly the long apple green shorts and loose blouse she was wearing, and bought just before going away, seemed dull and lifeless. Worse, they seemed positively ugly in their formless bagginess and lack of style.

'I don't know if it would suit me.'

'You don't have to buy. Just try it for fun.'

So she did. And when she emerged from the back room to look at herself in the long mirror in the shop she was pleased by how it enhanced her beauty with its slim lines. But the young woman looked very perturbed.

'Can I say something? You shouldn't wear underwear with this dress, not if you want it to have its full effect - if you know what I mean. After all, what is the point of buying a see-through dress if there is nothing to see?'

And here she gave a knowing laugh. Connie found herself laughing with her, and agreed to try it without, at least in the privacy of the shop.

And the young woman was right. Once naked underneath, she could see the full beauty and shape of her breasts. Her pubic hair, being light, was only the tiniest of suggestions between her legs. And when she turned she could see the strangely gorgeous, inviting curve of her buttocks below her hair, with the even more inviting groove between them. She was excited and disturbed by what she saw.

'Now you are beautiful. And, what's more important, erotic. These,' (the young woman held up her shorts), 'excuse me, but they do nothing for you. Give them to the poor at the first opportunity.'

Connie bought the dress.

Preparing to go out for dinner, she knew she wanted Stavros. She would have her demon lover, here on the Greek island where things could be safely contained, and left behind at the end of the holiday. But how, she didn't know. Maybe the dress would somehow drive him to it. Putting it on, she had a vision of her giving him an inviting look, and leaving Michael talking with a fisherman, going for a walk in the darkness along the beach. The moon would be full and hang, huge and sultry, just over the ocean. There would be a silver pathway across the rippling water. There would be a touch on her arm and it would be Stavros, his work finished for the night, and the two of them would stand there for many moments enchanted by the magic of the scene. He would refer to Shakespeare and other poets and his learning and his sensitivity would surprise her, and she would seek out his lips, which would be reluctant at first, but soon, through the insistence of her own, yielding to his desire, and the dress, so flimsy in its construction, would be torn off almost unnoticed, as they made passionate love right there on the edge of the Aegean, with the water gently lapping around them.

'Seen the binoculars?'

It was Michael entering the bedroom. He hardly glanced at her.

'On the table'

'*Kaiki* coming in. Must give her the once over. Been out fishing most likely.'

He was about to go out.

'What do you think?'

'What?'

'The dress.'

'Oh'

The slightest of glances.

'Fine.'

Then, shouted from the other room: 'I'm not changing for tonight. You notice the Greek fishermen don't. Just wear the grubby old stuff they've had on for weeks. Don't even shave.'

She decided to wear the dress, and without underwear. Stavros, she knew, would definitely have changed and be shaved.

They walked to the taverna, she aware of what an extraordinary couple they must make - he so dishevelled, and she so beautifully dressed and half naked. Full of expectation she entered the taverna only to discover that it was Stavros's day off. His young sister of twelve was serving in his place.

They ate in silence. Then the usual crew of locals arrived, and this time it was Michael who played host, offering rounds from the brandy bottle. She let them get on with it, only smiling or offering a word when she had to.

Suddenly she became aware that a fishing trip was proposed, specially for Michael. Andreas was challenging him in some way and he was responding. It was to do with seamanship, and there were looks and nudges going round the group, everyone watching to see how Michael would respond. Andreas was a fisherman who in the daytime took tourists out in his boat to different beaches. He was to take Michael out in his boat. Michael would bring it back. They would steer only by the stars. She could see that to Michael it was an incredible opportunity, not only to prove himself before these men, but to actually sail a traditional *kaiki*. What a story it would make back at the yacht club!

Yet there was something she wasn't happy about. They were manipulating him. They'd figured him out. They knew what his weakness was and were deliberately leading him. When he accepted the challenge looks of triumph went round. Yet also looks of fun and enjoyment: she could see they genuinely liked Michael. They were falling as much under his spell as he under theirs.

It was all arranged and it would be that night.

Apparently it had to be now or never: the boat was ready, the sea was ready. If he was a man, he must do it. Suddenly she saw that he was now almost indistinguishable from the others. He was even coming out with odd words of Greek. He, too, then, had his fantasy and was trying to live it. Of course women weren't allowed, this was man's business. She had been virtually ignored all evening.

There was a quick explanation from Michael.

'You can see yourself home, can't you, dear?'

She nodded, and they left together, laughing and joking, with more brandy. She followed them down to the quayside. They all jumped into Andreas's boat, and soon were chugging their way into the blackness. She was alone. Or was she? She realised that a figure was standing a little way off, just out of the lamplight, also watching the boat.

It was Stavros.

She stood, feeling embarrassed now, not sure what to do. Far from wanting to be brutally raped in the toilet, what she wanted now was to be safely locked in their little villa. Fantasies were one thing, reality something else. What would Stavros be thinking, seeing her dressed as she was? Surely he would draw his own conclusions. She would have to pass him on the way back. It was dark, no one was about, so forcing his attentions on her would be the easiest thing in the world... she walked in his direction. There was plenty of space, but somehow she contrived to direct her steps so she would pass close to him. He turned as she approached.

'*Kalispera.*'

'*Kalispera.*' Her voice came out thick, almost a whisper.

Was he going to pounce on her now? Carry her off? Do it to her here in the blackness? He stood there and did nothing. He clearly needed prompting.

'I'm on my own tonight.'

'I see it.'

Still he did nothing.

'Do you like my dress?'

'It's lovely.'

'Thankyou. It's a bit over the top.'

'A woman such as you can wear such a dress. Me, I would look silly in it.'

She laughed, and relaxed.

'I buy you a drink, yes?'

'I should go home.'

It was important to give at least the appearance of modesty.

'Of course, but first a little ouzo. I know a very nice little bar, very romantic, very quiet. And then I take you home.'

'OK.'

They walked a few metres along the ill-lit promenade. Would he do something? He could make his move, do anything he liked, she was at his mercy. As they came to a particularly dark patch, she suddenly felt his hand again, as she had done in the taverna, first casually stroking her buttocks then her hair. His touch was so light it was no more than a caress. She hardly dared breathe. Then his hand was under the hair, holding her gently at the nape of the neck as they walked. It was a strange feeling, this hold. No man had ever held her in this way before. It was a kind of taking possession. To be held there, right there in the vulnerable nape said to her 'You are mine'. The hold, so unmistakable, excited her.

She felt weak with desire, and, unable to walk further, stopped. She leaned against him and slipped her arms round him. She buried her face in his shirt, white, crisp and clean as she had expected. There was the scent of aftershave about him. He held her gently.

Then she was kissing him, deep and long, searching out his mouth with hers, and her own pressing passion forcing her to use hands and tongue immediately and shamelessly. Then his hands at last were all over her, and at last she was getting what she wanted and needed, rough, powerful caresses, first up into the hair, taking its full weight and length and then down her back, massaging her backside, then outrageously one was on her sex, through the thin cloth of the dress and she, with a squeal responding to it, clutching at the short, bristly hairs on his neck with one hand and at the back of his shirt with the other.

'Carry me.'

He seemed not understand.

'Pick me up. Lift. The beach. Take me to the beach.'

And then she was being lifted and carried in strong arms. How wonderful to be so powerless, literally swept off her feet!

He jumped the low wall of the promenade onto the beach and raced with her to the shore line, and placed her on the damp sand in front of a boat so they were concealed from the bars of the waterfront, their passion illuminated by the moon, not a full moon as she had imagined, it had a bit out of one side, but a moon nevertheless.

She realised he was fumbling with her dress.

'Rip it off!'

Again he didn't understand.

She made a tearing noise and motioned with her hands.

He kneeled astride her and took the top of her dress in both hands. With a sharp pull, it gave and tore right down the front. He bent to her breasts, kissing and kneading them, she gasping and giving stifled cries as her body responded, sending orgasmic waves sweeping away all thought. Then he had unzipped his fly, thrust his erect penis towards her mouth, at the same time forcing her head towards it. There was no choice, she must do the thing she always dreaded, had denied to Michael so firmly in the early days before he had given up asking. With moans of joy she sucked on the hard enormity of it, glorying in the ridges of the head and the feel of the starting veins while he massaged over and over the thickness of her hair, giving his own cries of ecstasy now.

Then she was forced back, the dress was brutally ripped right in half, and he was in her, thrusting with vigorous animal energy as she orgasmed almost instantly in her need, and then again and again, with unashamed gasps and cries before he came too, and he was out and lying gasping on the sand beside her.

She didn't smoke, but she shared a cigarette with him, and he took off his shirt and gave it to her to wear as a dress. Then laughing they went to the bar, just like that, she in his shirt and he stripped to the waist, to drink ouzo. And no one noticed, no one at all, only the bar girl, a brassy bleached blonde with an enormous false cleavage, who gave him a knowing look, and after a short exchange, a bunch of keys. Then they slipped out the back and up some stairs to a tiny room above the bar. It was beautifully clean and very feminine, with a single bed in one corner - small, but quite big enough if you wanted to be in a lover's arms.

'She hardly uses the room - sleeps with her man every night.'

Then she stripped him, put him on the bed, and made slow, long love to him glorying in the brown, young body, and sucking out his juices till she was satisfied and he dead to the world, giving in return the treasures of her own beauty, her big, big breasts and long, long golden hair.

And when he slept, she realised that even a demon lover

has limits, and might in reality only be a rather ordinary young man, but enjoyable for all that.

She returned early the next morning to the villa, and had plenty of time to create an air of normality before Michael returned with tales of his adventures the night before. It seemed it had been a success, but only because of his contribution and seamanship. He had found himself competent among fishermen who knew all there was to know about the sea. Mutual respect had been the outcome. And tonight there was to be a celebration, with some of the catch being cooked for them at the taverna.

'*Psarósoupa*,' he said. 'Fish soup. The fish is boiled with vegetables to make the stock, which is then made into a soup which you eat with the fish. They tell me it's delicious. Maybe you could wear that dress you bought.'

She had to think fast.

'Oh, that. It was rubbish. On the way home last night I took a walk on the beach, and it caught on something and tore right across. Had to throw it away. Stavros happened to be going by and lent me his shirt. He bought me a drink. He was a perfect gentleman.'

'Good show. Pity about the dress, though. Have to get you a new one. I want you to look beautiful. See-through, wasn't it?'

So he *had* noticed. With a shock, she realised this was a new Michael. But then, she was a new Connie.

3. The Feast

'You'll like it.'

'What festival is this?'

'*Ayios Mamas*'

'What's that?'

'It's the name of a saint. Anyway, that's not important. What is, though, is that it's really a pre-christian fertility rite. It's a tradition handed down from the old days. And by old days I mean very old, not just pre-christian but almost prehuman. We're talking dawn of man and all that.'

'You're pulling my leg.'

'Not at all. The tradition on our island is, that just once a year, on the eve of *Ayios Mamas*, a Vestal Virgin is chosen from among the young women of the island, and during the ancient rite she may choose any eligible man she likes from among the handsome male strangers specially assembled, and have it off with him. Then after that, all the woman can join in and have it with anyone they like. And the islanders still observe the tradition - even though, now the tourists have arrived, they don't need to. But Greeks like their traditions, you see. It's one of the things that kept us going during centuries of slavery.'

'And I'm one of the handsome strangers, I suppose.'

'Exactly. It's why I invited you here. Spending a month writing was a trick. All over the island families have been thinking up excuses to lure handsome strangers to the island. And then, tonight, we take them up into the mountains to the tiny isolated church of *Ayios Mamas*, where the rite will be enacted.'

'I don't believe it.'

'I know I've told you some awful whoppers at times but this one is absolutely true, as God is my witness.'

'You're an atheist.'

'OK, I swear by the name of Karl Marx.'

'But why?'

'New seed. Don't you see? Small island, very isolated, inter-marriage, loads of half-wits. Got to find a way of keeping up the strength of the stock, and what better way than to invite a load of people and have a party?'

George was more serious than David would have liked. He didn't want to become some kind of guinea pig in an ancient ceremony in which who knows what happened. Anything was possible in this place, he'd already sensed that, and he'd only been here two days. It had a wild chaos about it that was not redolent of the England of Oxford University. They were both PhD students working in the same laboratory on roughly the same problem of genetic engineering. They had started together and now, after three years of research, in which they had discovered one or two entirely uninteresting items of data, were writing their theses. George had suggested they retire to his ancestral home on a Greek island. His mother was Greek, and belonged to a noble family with property on the island. It had seemed the ideal place, so they had set off.

The mansion had proved to be everything George had cracked it up to be. It was situated in an olive grove and was built like a fortress - basically a square stone tower with tiny windows and walls of immense thickness. However, this made it pleasantly cool inside. The family had long since moved to England and now used it only for holidays, but it had serviceable, ancient furniture, a large balcony stretching the whole length of the house and looking out to sea, and a beach nearby. They intended to swim and write, and have long talks over vast quantities of ouzo, wine and beer. Food was to be eaten at the taverna on the beach. A woman from the nearest cottage, half a kilometre away, was to come to clean.

Distractions like this festival were not part of the plan, especially before they'd even got properly started.

'Why don't we get on with the work for tonight? We can party later.'

'It will put you in the mood. Give birth to your creativity - these ancient celebrations are about contacting the deep unconscious, liberating its power.'

David was sceptical.

'So what exactly happens at this supposed fertility festival?'

'Ah. Now that's very interesting. It starts with music and dancing. And then there's a feast - you know, lamb on the spit and all that traditional Greek stuff, and to go with it, wine. But this isn't ordinary wine, it's retsina, made to a very special recipe, handed down from generation to generation. It contains a combination of resin and herbs collected from the mountainside, that makes it a drug with interesting psychedelic properties.'

'So everyone gets high. So what?'

'Ah, but they don't. Not the women. Only the men. The women hardly drink at all, they just ply the men with more and more. And the women hardly eat either, not unless specially offered a choice morsel by a man. And she is fed by him, straight into the mouth. Very erotic to watch. And the feasting goes on for some time, with much jollity all round. And then, as the meal comes to an end, the music changes. It is hardly noticeable at first, but becomes more and more insidious. And it's that strange Greek music that you sometimes hear by chance but can never quite find out where it's coming from. You know, the stuff that sort of lingers and whines, seems to come from the Orient, perhaps, but it also has a primitive air to it like it goes back thousands of years to the time before there was music and Pan blew on his pipes, and Satyrs danced, half animal, half human. And egged on by the women, the men start dancing an erotic, primitive dance that comes from somewhere deep inside, whose steps they don't have to learn because they know them already, a drunken, psychedelic dance in which they lose touch with reality. It goes on and on, and finally they strip off their clothes, and form a circle of linked arms with at its centre the Vestal Virgin. And they dance round her. And she too is naked and dances a snake-like dance, tempting them, driving them on, showing all her charms, until they are mad with desire, and their erections are so enormous they hurt. And in her hand is an apple, just like from the garden of Eden, and she takes a bite from it, then offers it first to one and then another of the men, only to take it away again until finally - she chooses. She stops in front of a man, takes big bite, and offers it to him. And if he accepts, he takes the apple and bites into it, too, before falling on her, right there in the middle of the circle, and deflowering her. And all this time the other women have been watching and are stone cold sober and can now snatch the man of their choice, drag him into the bushes and have him. And of course the men are so drunk, all of them, husbands, lovers, strangers, they don't know what's happening. And in the morning not one of them is any the wiser. Of course the women are, because they've been orchestrating the whole thing, but they keep their secret. And so does *Agios Mamas*, who's been watching from on high, with a smile and a blessing. And of course, the happy couple, the Vestal Virgin and her chosen man, get married later and have hordes of children and live happily ever after.'

David felt stunned, somehow drawn in by the whole narration.

'Got you! Ha! Done it again! You're too easy.'

David felt himself coming sharply back to reality.

'You bastard.'

'Anyway, we're going to the festival this evening, bloody boring, bit of food and drink, but since I'm nobility and I'm in residence I have no choice but to attend. Get yourself washed and dressed for eight.'

And so it was that later that day David was being driven at a break-neck speed through the rapidly darkening countryside in the family Beetle. After a while, the road became little more than a track, with wild flowers and bushes on either side, leaning so far over as to scrape both sides of the vehicle and fill it with wild country scents.

Other cars were ahead and behind them, all racing in the same direction. Suddenly George screeched to a halt, narrowly avoiding hitting the car in front, which had stopped, and the car behind did the same.

'This is where we get out. End of the line.'

They got out and all around David could see dim shadows also getting out of their cars. Following everyone else, they walked along the track a short distance, before turning off the road and following a path that climbed up and up through a dark pine forest. After a while, David began to discern lights far above them, high up on the mountain. By the time they reached them and entered a brightly lit churchyard full with people, they were sweating.

He felt very much a guest and very English at this gathering. It was quite different from George's story. Everyone seemed very prim and proper, and reserved. The band, which was on a small dais, was made up of faces he recognised: the man from the bank, the man from the post office, and so on. To his surprise they struck up a foxtrot: very Greek in style, but still recognisable. Older people were dancing sedately in couples.

'It's the island national dance. We took it over from the British when they left.'

Suddenly David gasped. A young woman came up to George, and in a most alluring manner, without saying anything, swept him off into the dance. What affected him so much was the way she was dressed. Though not particularly pretty, she was tall and slim, and made the most of it by wearing a pure white dress, sleeveless and backless, cut so short it finished somewhere just below the crotch. And it was so tight that her shapely bottom stuck out at the rear, her shapely breasts stuck out at the front, and her shapely hips stuck out at the sides. Her skin was smooth and kissed by the sun to a dark, chocolate brown. He wanted her and was jealous.

But not for long. A new lust was almost immediately presented to him. A young woman whom he recognised from the village, came up to offer him a drink. If anything, her appearance was more outrageous. Taking the drink, he couldn't help staring, open-mouthed. What she had done with herself was completely different, but no less appealing - she had on tight torn jeans and T shirt that displayed bits of her slim body in the most tantalisingly unexpected places. And he couldn't help being turned on by the way the jeans had been designed to hang low over the hips and dipped down at the front so as to expose a huge expanse of pretty navel. But she only smiled, stroked his cheek, and walked away, her ample, rounded backside swaying generously. It seemed to invite a pinch. But he very properly resisted the impulse. However, an elderly gentleman, smartly dressed in a dark suit, to whom she next offered a drink, was clearly unable to resist and gave her a good one as she turned away. And far from scolding him, the young woman seemed delighted, and gave him a broad smile and a wave.

Then he became aware that more and more young women were arriving, and all had done outrageous things to themselves. Were they prostitutes? It was impossible. And how did the sedate older folks allow it? They seemed to be taking no notice. The foxtrot stopped and became a waltz, and then Greek music started, popular dances that everyone seemed to know, and the little square became a throng of people dancing in circles and enjoying themselves.

And everywhere, weaving their way among the throng were these alluring young women, each dressed more outrageously than than the next - one was wearing nothing but plastic, another leather, someone else a dress so see-through she might just as well have been wearing nothing.

Looking at these young women David's eyes felt scalded. Yet they seemed so cool and confident in their outrageousness, as if it was the most natural thing in the world. It must be, David assured himself, a difference in culture. It's what a young woman was expected to do here.

He realised that they'd all obviously heard the story George had told, because when his glass was next given a top-up by a young woman, she had winked and said 'very special brew this'. And yes it had seemed very strong and sweet, and thick, almost like oil, very different from the bottled retsina he was used to. And when other young women came up to fill his glass, which they did frequently, they all winked too.

And looking round a little later, they were very generous, he realised, the young women serving, and he made efforts to hold back, because he didn't want a thick head in the morning. Nothing must interfere with the work. But it was difficult. They were so sly, the way they filled your glass, and somehow it slipped down so easily. But he managed to maintain limits, by some sly tricks of his own, spilling the odd glass by accident, pretending to drink when he wasn't, and pouring the remainder into George's glass. He noticed that there did seem to be a number of guests like himself, clearly Northern European, and all male. There didn't seem to be any foreign women: all the women looked decidedly and unmistakably Greek. And no children. Now that was odd. In past visits to Greece, children had always been in evidence, at all communal events, even very late at night. And the women, while they did put glasses to their lips, hardly seemed to drink, just sip at it, just to keep the men company - or perhaps it was an illusion.

However, despite these observations, David felt relaxed and at peace. It was early September, the weather was warm, very still, and they were gathered outside, in a tiny country churchyard, surrounded by pines. There was the scent of resin in his nostrils and pine needles under his feet. He idly and contentedly watched the lamb turn on the spit. It was true that the wine did have a very dreamy effect...

That was when he first saw her, a young woman so beautiful, it went beyond his wildest dreams. She was arriving with her father, who was jolly and fat and definitely the life and soul of the party. He went round greeting everyone with the traditional greeting of *Hrónia Pollá!* and laughingly shaking hands, including David's.

But the daughter greeted no one - simply sat down next to a girl friend and started talking. David felt a keen disappointment. He was already attracted to her. Their eyes had met when she first arrived, and they had been deep brown, large, and wonderful. She had looked round the room checking who was there, and had taken in all the guests, including David. And now her every movement had a slight theatrical quality to it, as if she knew she was the focus of attention, and was desired by all the men present.

What was the magic? He wasn't sure. She was dressed more modestly than the other young women, but nevertheless fashionably. The first thing he had noticed about her was her hair - thickly abundant and chestnut brown, parted in the middle and falling in a glossy mass to just above her shoulders where it was carefully turned under - the effect of this studied styling being to make it seem more full and thick than if it had been allowed to grow freely.

She had on a simple white jumper, from which poked two ample breasts, which, while not alot was made of them, nevertheless were full ones. Yes, fullness, that was all you could say - a full, pretty face, with full cheeks, a full smile, full, bright, brown eyes. Everything about her was full - but in no way fat, as was the father. No, she was studiously slim in the right places, with a delightfully pinched waistline leading to full hips from which vantage point dangled a leather miniskirt so fashioned as to pertly emphasise, without loss of modesty, the full, rounded shape of her backside.

Below it were two strong legs, those perhaps of a swimmer, or at least someone prepared to muck in to some hard work, but again, not fat, just full, and delightfully finishing in dainty feet.

She was attractive, no doubt about it. Ready, somehow, very ready, but for what? Life, perhaps. Love perhaps. A ripe fruit, full and juicy, waiting to be picked. Oh to taste her! And what would she taste of? Surely sugar and spice and all things nice - Greek style, of course.

In his obsession with her, David had not noticed George return:

'Sou Arési?'

'What?'

'Does she please you?'

'She's lovely.'

'She's a Vestal Virgin if ever there was one. Her name's Virginia, pronounced *Veeryinéea.* She's the village beauty. You see this jar?'

David made an effort to look away from Virginia.

'Aha.'

It was an antique earthenware jar, chest high, and almost as fat.

'Her father says he wants a man for her who can fill this jar with money.'

'Well, I can't. Wish I could.'

Suddenly the lamb was removed from the smouldering fire, and everyone sat down at long wooden tables. David found himself with George on one side and by a happy coincidence, opposite Virginia, with her father next to her. Large platters of meat and vegetables were placed in front of them.

'Here, try some of this.'

George thrust some rather odd looking bits of brown under his nose. He picked one and bit into it. It was strangely spongy.

'What is it?'

'Lungs.'

David suppressed a desire to vomit and smiled weakly, but George had already turned away to talk to a friend.

He looked at Virginia but she was being occupied by a girl friend on her other side. Then he caught the eye of the father opposite. Things were said in Greek that he couldn't understand, but he gathered that the father wanted to communicate.

The man sitting next to him translated.

'He says he understands you are from Oxford University.'

'Yes. I am.'

'He doesn't trust the English teacher at the school. His daughter here isn't progressing as she should. He wants you to give her a few lessons. If you would be so kind. He knows you must have important work to do.'

Lessons with Virginia! What a wonderful idea! He felt warm and amenable. True there was the thesis to write - but Virginia!

'Of course.'

An agreement was made, exactly what, he couldn't quite follow, but found himself going with the flow. He made a conscious effort to pour the wine away. If he wasn't careful, things would get out of hand. In fact, all around him, things did seem to be.

The daughter in question was at this moment having a long piece of roasted meat held above her head by an admirer who laughingly dangled it into her mouth, and she was biting bits off in the most sensual way imaginable. It was like the party game in England with apples on strings, but so much more erotic. Her eyes were bright and shining, and she was behaving lovingly towards it, kissing it, licking it, sucking on it, before it was dropped in, chewed, and swallowed. Looking round, other young women were having the same done to them. Everyone was having such fun. He felt reserved and shy, and very English. He would have to make a better show: when in Rome...

He swallowed some wine and boldly took a long sliver of juicy meat from a huge plate on the table, and holding his breath, stood up, leant over the table towards Virginia, who was free at that moment, and dangled, too. He met the girl's eyes, and as she accepted the offering and ate, the gaze held. Then he fed her with another piece, and another.

Then she was indicating to him to sit down and talking to him.

'I would so love to be a teacher' she was saying, in halting, but nice English. They conversed pleasantly. He liked her. A little friendship sprang up. Realising she was to be his student, he tried to retain a little formality, but found he couldn't. She was so winning. She had him laughing with her in no time.

Then a very strange thing happened. The meal was over, so it seemed, and people sat back. There was an air of expectancy. Then he noticed that the music had changed and a new type had been playing for some time, gradually increasing in volume. It was a kind of wail, hardly music at all, clearly Greek, with an Oriental flavour, yet also the flavour of the earth itself. He looked round for the musicians but could see none, presumably they had hidden themselves for reasons of their own.

Then suddenly Virginia broke off what she was saying, got up and walked across the churchyard and towards the gate. There must have been some kind of signal.

At the gate she turned to look at David, then was gone.

He was disappointed. Was it bedtime already?

The father had got up and was dancing with one of the sexily-dressed young women, waggling his huge stomach at her, his bottom, his arms, everything, laughing hugely, and there were cheers from the onlookers, and the young woman was egging him on, and then inviting other men to join in, which they did, rotating themselves alarmingly at her. And more men joined in, Greek at first, including George, and more women egged them on, and some men were stripping off their shirts because of the heat. A big Swede with mountains of blond hair joined in, stripping to his underpants, and looking magnificent and muscular. Then other Northern-looking men joined him, more weedy, but nevertheless stripping down too.

And then it was David's turn. He was being invited. He plunged in, and suddenly all the men were at it, in a great circle, all dancing to the same drone that just went on and on, compulsively, as if there was nothing to stop it. And the women now got very saucy - one pulled down the underpants of the Swede, so he was naked, but he submitted and stepped out of them gaily. David noticed that the Swede had an erection, but he didn't seem to care, and nor did anyone else. Then the women stripped another man, and another. They both had erections. But still no one cared. There was only the dance and the music and the circle of men, and it was wonderful, and then again it was David's turn to be laughingly stripped, and he too had an erection, and he didn't care either. And then they were all naked, and they all had huge erections, and were proudly displaying them. And they danced a male dance going back centuries, eons, it was male bonding, but a bonding so deep it was like a pain, a beautiful pain, it was love, there were tears in his eyes, joy at belonging to the community of men and he wished it could go on forever, but of course it had and it would and under his feet were pine needles, and it was as if they were dancing on a huge bed, and around him the men seemed scarcely human any more, more like satyrs, and he could swear they had tails.

And then a startling thing. The men weren't dancing alone any more. In their midst was a young woman. And it wasn't any young woman, it was Virginia, and she was naked, and she was writhing her young body, so surprisingly pale in this sun-kissed place, like she had been deliberately kept out of the sun for this very occasion, dancing a virgin's dance for the men, showing herself to them.

And David felt his desire rising and becoming more and more powerful and his erection growing, bigger and bigger until it hurt, and he was baying for her, as the other men around him were baying.

Then he saw that she had an apple, green and large, from which she took a huge bite, and she began tantalisingly snaking up to one man and offering the apple, only to snatch it away again, and the baying reached a peak of frenzy as she offered it to man after man before finally focussing on - David.

He found himself thrust into the centre.

There was silence.

He was being offered the apple. He knew what he had to do. He took it and bit it, taking a large bite from the other side, before casting it away.

And Virginia was dancing only for him now, in the silence. She was writhing herself, pulsating her hips, waggling her breasts at him, driving him on, until, there she was, on her back, legs splayed, on the pine needles before him, ready, inviting him in with her arms.

He felt so powerful, so male, so strong, so animal.

In a moment he was on her, forcing his cock into her. And as he did so the silence around him exploded into manic screams, people were running, falling, there were naked bodies writhing all around, but he was focussed only on Virginia. He was thrusting and thrusting and she was gasping his name with each thrust:

'David, David, David!'

And then suddenly the semen was pulsing, and he was glorying in each fertilising pulse, and the woman was receiving with gasps of joy and satisfaction:

'D-a-v-i-d!!'

And then he was back home in bed.

At least he thought it was bed. How had he got there? He wasn't sure. But somehow it had happened. Here he was, in bed. Someone must have helped him. He opened his eyes. Yes, bed. There were his clothes neatly folded on a chair.

An image of pine needles and dancing, nakedness and copulation came back. Had it been a dream? He wasn't sure. Maybe he'd had more than he'd thought. More care next time. But he had no headache, he felt dreamy, between waking and sleeping, and that was nice. Must have been good wine, even if it was a mite strong.

The girls had been so beautiful, and especially Virginia, and he had an image of Virginia taking the meat from him with her mouth: yes, that had happened, certainly. But had they really taken off their clothes and danced, had he really...?

'David.'

Had she really chosen him and had he...?

'David'

He opened his eyes again. That last David had sounded very real.

He had another image, now, of her, naked as the night before, not writhing in a sensual dance, but natural, standing in the doorway with a tray.

He opened his eyes wider. He blinked.

The image did not go away. The image spoke and the English was better than it was yesterday. Much better. It came towards the bed.

'David. Hello. You woke up.'

The voice was sweet and delightful to him. So was the warm, easy smile. So were the brown eyes, the full breasts, the ample hips.

It was real. It was her. She was in the room.

He sat up.

'I brought you breakfast.'

On the tray were two delicious-smelling mugs of coffee

and little squares of toast, *friganyés,* covered in marmalade. In the middle of the tray, the centre-piece, a large green apple with two bites out of it.

He realised that he was very hungry.

She put it on the bed by him.

'Virginia.'

'*Veeryinéea*'

'Why are you here?'

'It's time for my English lesson.'

She said it slyly as if it involved a shared secret. He drank some coffee and bit into a piece of toast.

Then she did a surprising thing, as if being there was not surprising enough. Perfectly naturally, as if she had been doing it for forty years, she lifted the sheet and got in beside him. It was a large double bed, very old, made of metal with metal springs, and it squeaked. She took her mug of coffee and sipped at it. She smiled at him.

'Virginia, you mustn't.'

'Mustn't what?'

'Do this. We're supposed to be having lessons.'

'I don't need lessons. My English is very good.' Then a little doubt in her voice. 'You want me, don't you?'

'Yes of course I want you.'

'So why not?'

He couldn't think why not. She was young. She was beautiful. He liked her. He was young. He was beautiful (well, fairly, if you took a generous perspective and ignored the persistent spots and the rather weedy physique). She liked him.

'What about your father?' he asked rather lamely.

'What about your father?'

'*Touche.*'

He sat eating his toast and drinking his coffee, and so did

she. He realised he was accepting it. But he should be resisting. There was a feeling of the solid ground of Oxfordshire slipping away from beneath his feet. It was being replaced with a treacherous chaos of pine needles. He couldn't trust anything any more. But what was he to do? Jump out of bed? He didn't want to.

He took her empty cup, put the tray aside, and turned to her. She was still chewing. Her mouth was full, and a little bit of marmalade was on her cheek. He wiped it off with a finger and put it to her lips. She took the finger in her mouth and sucked off the marmalade. Then she swallowed and laughed.

He tried her name the proper way.

'*Veeryineea.*'

She laughed.

'Not bad. I must teach you Greek. *Yasoo* David. That means hello.'

'*Yasoo.*'

She was marvellous. He couldn't believe his luck. And such a beauty. He stroked the cool, heavy tresses of her hair. Then he was kissing her gently on the mouth, feeling the soft fullness of her lips...

His penis hardened, and embarrassed, he pulled away, glancing down. She saw the movement of his eyes and putting a hand under the covers, found the offending member.

'So you do still want me.'

'Oh yes.'

Then she was under the covers and her warm mouth was around it, hardening it and exciting it with her tongue, he wanted it to go on and on, but suddenly she was out again, laughing.

'You like it?'

'Very much.'

Then impulsively he was under the covers, doing a similar thing to her, fumbling a bit in his inexperience. Of course he knew in principle what to do, he'd heard of the clit, and fingered the odd girl friend. She tasted of almonds. Then instructions were being firmly issued from above.

'Up a bit. Bit more. There. Gently with the tongue. Up and down, slowly at first then getting faster. Ah! Yes! Oh yes! *Christé mou!*'

She pulled his head away and he came out from under, and they were kissing again, and he was feeling the gorgeous silky smoothness of her body, with its strong thighs, and he was fumbling with his penis to find her entrance, and she lifted it and manoeuvring it expertly so it went in easily, and then they were rolling, with him on top of her, then her on top of him, and then suddenly, looks of surprise on both sides.

'I'm coming I'm sorry'.

'Come! come! I'm coming too'!

They came.

And then there was a moment's pleasure of looking into the deep brown eyes in ecstacy, and staying with them as their bodies eased down.

She sat up and peeled the apple. She cut slices and they shared it. And then she was looking at the clock on the bedside table.

'I must go. Lesson's over. See you tomorrow.'

And she was out of bed, and gone.

He felt relaxed, marvellous. Ready for work.

And so the month passed. He didn't say much to George about Virginia. He was absorbed in his own writing and didn't seem to want to know. He knew she was coming for lessons, of course, but never inquired about them.

Two days before their departure, David's thesis was written up, and George's still in a complete mess. For some reason he couldn't seem to get anywhere with it. David was at a loose end and wanted to do something special with Virginia, something that would be a leaving present. Could she arrange it so that her ever-watchful father wouldn't know? She had said she could. She would say she was making a *paréa* with some girlfriends. They would cover for her, no problem. It was something she often did.

They decided to walk to a secret gorge Virginia knew, with a stream running even in the height of summer.

Setting off at the appointed time, they walked for perhaps an hour, first along a track David knew, then they cut inland along a path he hadn't noticed before. Soon, high cliffs of rock were rising above them on both sides, and they joined a stream with water running in it, under the canopy of trees that protected it and turned the banks into a steamy jungle. Here there was a footpath between enormous plants, bursting with flowers. Large yellow butterflies fluttered from blossom to blossom.

They found a green, open place, and spent the day eating and drinking from the basket of food Virginia had brought, and of course making delicious love. Between bouts they went for walks along the stream banks, and found little frogs, freshwater crabs and a snake, and the many-coloured butterflies, all in huge abundance even so late in the year, accompanied them everywhere.

When they returned home, arm in arm, David was surprised to find others going their way, who silently joined them. First the man who did the garden, to whom he said hello, but there was no reply, so they continued. Then the old woman who cleaned the house popped out from behind a bush, then more people. All along the way they collected people. By the time they got to the house it was a silent party of about twelve. The atmosphere was strained. David realised that something was wrong, it had to do with him and Virginia, but he brazened it out.

As they approached the house, David saw Virginia's father with a shotgun over his arm, sounding very angry, remonstrating with George outside the door. When the father saw David, he came rushing up to him, shouted something at him, and hit him squarely on the jaw. David fell, more in surprise than anything, because, although the man was huge, his aim was off and most of the force had gone from the blow. However, the wonderful Virginia came down to console him with her arms so it was worth making more of it.

The shotgun was then cocked, raised, and aimed.

George explained in unexpectedly calm tones.

'It seems you've been a naughty boy. You've been fucking his daughter for some weeks now and the expected proposal of marriage has not been forthcoming. Unless you agree to marry her right now he will kill you. Both of you.'

David's reaction was instantaneous: after all, he was British.

'Tell him he's welcome to kill me, but spare the girl.'

There was a moment of uncertainty as the outraged father turned to George for a translation.

George said something in Greek, there was a moment's argy-bargy, and then the man, after one more aiming of the gun, safely stowed it over his shoulder. George helped David up and they retired to the house.

'I told him to leave us alone for a bit so we could discuss the situation. After all, you're not going anywhere, there's only one door to this place and he can kill you anytime.'

'We must call the police.'

'I don't think that will help much in this case. The chief of police is one of the outraged populace outside. You see, you've broken a rule. You've had a vestal virgin. Not only had her, but had her over and over again.'

David was aghast.

'How do you know?'

'Everyone knows. They all know everything in this place. You've been seen. They told me.'

'She was in my private room.'

'There's no such thing as a private room here. It has windows, doesn't it? You were even seen at the gorge today, among the butterflies. There were some very unusual positions.'

'We were alone.'

'You thought you were alone. That's different.'

'So they knew and they did nothing about it?'

'They had their reasons. We're coming to that. You're allowed to look but you're not allowed to have. Not unless you intend marriage. That's the rule. It's tradition. Punishment is death for both of you.'

'Why both of us? I can see why he's angry with me. OK, I shouldn't have done it, not in a traditional place like this, but this is the modern world. People have rights. I have rights.'

'Ah, but that's just it. He has rights - rights of tradition. She has disgraced the family. So, even if you were to escape, she must die.

'We must do something!'

'Don't worry, she's safe for now, I got a stay of execution. Just say you'll marry her.'

'I don't want to. Not under pressure. I'm not ready for marriage. I need time. I'm still a student, I don't even have a proper job. You said he wants a man who can fill that jar with money. There's no way I could fill that jar. I'm not even eligible.'

'Ah, but you are. Look at it from his point of view. OK, so you're not rich. But you're a good investment. You may not be able to fill the jar now but you will be able to. You're at Oxford University, you've been very successful up to now, you've even completed your thesis, and anyway you're English and that puts you in the ruling class. You represent safety. He's still a peasant, basically, the man is ignorant. Any learning he has, has been cobbled together by his own wits and guts. Which are considerable. So let's not underestimate him.'

'Why an Englishman? Why not choose a Turk, or an Italian? They've all ruled here. The French for that matter.'

'Not a Turk. Definitely not. Not acceptable on any score. And yes, Venetians have been rulers here but an Italian is not the same as a Venetian.'

'An Italian from Venice, then.'

'Again, not the same thing. Venice died out, England didn't. As for the French, well, they were in the same boat as us during the last war. No, an Englishman is special. And Oxford University puts the stamp of authenticity on it. You're a certainty as far as investments go. Anyway, she wants you. I understand she chose you and you accepted her choice.'

'What do you mean?'

'She chose you at the *Agios Mamas* festival.'

More astonishing news.

'She what?'

'Was there a large green apple on your breakfast tray the morning after the *Agios Mamas* festival?'

'Yes. I think there was. We ate it.'

'The apple is the sign that you're the chosen by the Vestal Virgin. And if you eat it, it shows you accept. No other woman is now allowed to have you, until after you are married. Then they can, of course, once a year. And the women will observe that, communicate it, even to tourist women, and strangely enough, they will observe it too. The international club of women. Funny sometimes, seeing these chosen ones desperately trying to get off with girl after girl, not succeeding, and not understanding why. And then falling back on the only one who will let them. You might as well accept that you are now finished as far as other women are concerned. You might just as well agree.'

'She's not a virgin. She can't be, not with all that expertise.'

'She's a *de facto* virgin and traditionally that's the same thing.'

'What do you mean now? What's this new trick? David realised he was angry and at the end of his tether. He could not see how to get out of this. George was infuriatingly cool.

'It's not a trick. Obviously she's not a virgin in the ordinary sense. None of them are. Virginity is a social role. Like Bank Manager and Milkman. It's about things you do in society. They refrain from obvious sex. It has to be done discreetly with no one looking. Of course, someone's always looking, as you know. And these days no one would expect you to marry her simply on account of what happened at the *Agios Mamas* festival. There's got to be compatibility. You've got to be tested out in performance, so to speak, given a trial run.'

'Are you saying that's why she came to my bed the following morning?'

'You could say that.'

'You mean it's a set-up. You've set me up. All of you.'

'Not exactly. I see I'm going to have to be very honest with you, though.'

'It's about time.'

'I invited you here because I like you. And of course we had our theses to write. But if you're an islander, and I pride myself on being one by descent, then you are always on the lookout for doing a young woman a good turn. The father wrote to me. Did I know anyone? As it happened, I did. Someone very nice. I brought him here. It was just a matter of timing the visit. There was no question of setting you up. There were a whole lot of eligible young men at the festival. She could have chosen any of them. But she chose you.'

'Why don't *you* have her?'

'I can't because she's not of noble blood. She's a peasant.'

'Claptrap, bigoted claptrap.'

'As you wish. So: something you must understand about Greece. It is the home of the drama. Life itself is a kind of tragicomedy acted out for real. So in these events there is a ritual element.'

'More claptrap.'

'When she sleeps with you, she is not sleeping with you, she is making a point. When he aims a gun at you he is not aiming a gun he is making a point.'

'You mean the gun isn't loaded?'

'Oh I didn't say that. From time to time there have been unfortunate accidents. Only a couple of years ago, for instance, but the father was *very* traditional and a bit mad. And of course it's the risk the Vestal Virgin makes. If she chooses the wrong man and it doesn't work out, she loses her life. She knows that. Most of the time it never comes to that.'

'You mean they give in and marry the wench.'

'They see reason. I would never have taken you to the festival if I didn't think you were well matched. And obviously everyone else agreed with me or they wouldn't have allowed things to proceed, the drama to be acted out, if you like.'

'You traitor. You let me fall into this.'

'Not fall. Slide, perhaps. But very gently. With infinite care. There were moments when both of you acted strongly under your own initiative. We were merely the audience. We liked what we saw. It pleased us. In fact, we were thrilled that two such lovely people should find each other. However, now she's pregnant and it's time for the play to reach a satisfactory conclusion.'

'Pregnant?'

'She's told a girlfriend that her body is different. She can feel it inside. I take it you didn't use contraceptives?'

'I didn't think of it.'

'It speaks for itself. And after all that sex education. You could have given her something very nasty. Look on it as a kind of arranged marriage. Arranged for you by those around you who know about these things and want the best for both of you. Probably they know you better than you know yourself. And anyway you could always divorce her again later, the Greek church is very easy on such things. It's only the show of marriage that's important, the theatre, the social role of it. Don't see yourself as tied, more as acting a part.

'I'm not going to go into a shotgun marriage, and that's it.'

'You really don't want to?'

'No.'

'She is really very nice.'

'No.'

George was thoughtful.

'OK, perhaps I can get you out if you really don't want to. We may be able to negotiate something, but there are other issues involved that you don't know about. When I say he's making a point, he's saying that she's his property. In most cases you'd get away with a few shotgun pellets in your backside or its equivalent: honour has to be satisfied. Virginia, well, she would get away with losing her lovely hair for a while, that's traditional. But in this case an exchange will have to be made.'

'What sort of exchange?'

'Land. There's yet another angle on this. There are always angles in Greece, and, now I think about it, I can see that I may have been tricked. There's an olive grove up on the mountain that belongs to my family and ajoins his land. His family's wanted it since the time of the Turkish occupation. It was got, they think, by unfair dealing with the conquerors. Of course they'd unfairly got it from us before that, under the Venetians, but let that pass. And when the British were here the governor fudged the issue by assigning half to each of us, thus putting the deadly rivals side by side.'

'I can't let you give away olive groves on my account.'

'It's *Filoxenia*: Greek laws of hospitality. If you really, in your heart of hearts, don't want her, you are my guest and I am in honour bound to do so. As you rightly say, I got you into this. He knows that. I can see that I've been away too long. Living in England has made me naive. He's doing it for her and hers. It's clever. Looked at like that, there was no choice for Virginia. She had to have you, a friend of mine, that's why they got me to invite you. Yes, he's got us over a barrel. I hope an olive grove will do it, that's all.'

Suddenly David felt himself relenting to some degree. After all, if it was as he said, just an enactment, nothing permanent, why not? She would have to understand, of course, that it was not binding on either side, although he'd be prepared to give it a fair trial.

'Let me talk to her first and then give you my decision.'

He could see George was delighted, even though he tried to suppress it.

'You won't regret it. Think of it. Beautiful bride. Horde of glorious kids. And he'll build a house for you and yours in perpetuity - well, not forgetting that everything goes in the female line here, of course.'

There were always new angles, new rules.

'Let me see her.'

George was about to leave. David had a thought.

'It was an incredible experience, by the way. I never told you.'

'What?'

'*Agios Mamas*. Such intense male bonding, us dancing together, naked like that, erections and all. And then taking the virgin, you know, the basic ritual of deflowerment. Wonderful.'

George paled.

'You don't mean to say you remember some of it?'

'A bit. More than a bit. I held back on the wine.'

'You shouldn't have. That was very silly. Never say another word. Not to me. Or anyone else. And especially not Virginia. You know what they do to a Peeping Tom? The women band together and one night, when he's least expecting it, they tear him to pieces, limb from limb. And their final act is to tear out his heart and eat it. It has happened. It is written. And if you participate again in *Agios Mamas* again, drink. Drink heartily. It is forbidden for men to know.'

Then he was gone. Virginia appeared. She looked tousled, her eyes were swollen with crying, there was a bruise on one arm, but otherwise she was unharmed. She stood there looking at him. There was a rueful, guilty expression on her face. He looked at her.

She wasn't pretty anymore. Just ordinary. But did that matter? It didn't. It honestly didn't. She was not a virgin.

But then why should she be? Would he expect it of a young woman at home? Of course not. There was no transgression there. She was calculating. Scheming. She had used all her feminine arts outrageously and got what she wanted. Him. So what? She would carry on being calculating and scheming. But did that matter? No it didn't. It was a bit like waking up one morning and seeing a tousled head next to him, suffering from the flu. Seen at its worst. But loving it just the same. He realised that he *wanted* to wake up one morning and see her suffering from the flu. It was strange. To realise he loved her. And why not? They'd had a month together, and it had worked. There had been quicker whirlwind romances. And perhaps he *was* ready. Perhaps they *did* know him better than he knew himself.

He held out his hand for her. He kissed her. It was a long kiss. Then hand in hand they went out of the door.

There was cheering. There was joy. Of course. One drama was successfully concluded and another was beginning.

They got married in Greece among much feasting, with George as best man announcing to the gathered assembly that traditionally he had the right of *droit de seigneur* : to sleep with the bride on her wedding night. It was a law which had never been officially repealed. There had been a moment's silence. But then he'd laughed and said that tonight, as a special favour, he wasn't going to exercise it, so everyone had laughed and toasted the happy couple in a very English way.

Virginia's father built them a beautiful villa right near the top of a hill, glistening and white, surrounded on three sides by olive trees, its front looking out over a fertile valley towards the castle and out to the sea. It was their own olive grove, half given by Virginia's father, the other half by George, so in this way an ancient wrong was at last righted.

Tourists passing on the main road far below would look up with envy and wonder whose it was.

'The Englishman's' was the only answer they would receive.

George never married. Over time all the nobles had died out. He was the only one left, so there was no one suitable to marry. But, with the question of the olive grove finally settled, he made friends with the father and whenever he was on the island they would go hunting, shooting and fishing together, killing as many of God's most beautiful creatures as they possibly could, and really enjoying it.

And David was able to fill the jar, metaphorically speaking, perhaps twice over. And in later years George always used to laugh that, in David's household, full of young daughters who would eventually need partners, there was only one person who wore the trousers and it wasn't David. He did exercise his right over the bride on one occasion, from curiosity on both sides after not a little wine, but it didn't work out and it was never repeated.

And as far as I know David kept his secret and never did tell anyone about what happened at the festival of *Ayios Mamas*. Just as well. You never know.

4. Kamaki

In the Greek language, the word 'kamaki' refers to the skill of seducing women, and a man who devotes his life to the seduction of women is called a 'kamaki'. Many Greek men pride themselves on their talents in this area. On the island, Andreas was the acknowledged pastmaster - the kamaki to beat all kamakis. A Kamaki, however, cannot forever deny the passage of time. Beauty fades. We grow older and the urge diminishes, however slightly. There comes a moment when even the most skilful kamaki must yield to younger successors.

Seduction was the last thing on Andreas's mind as he entered the bar. It was one of those days at the height of summer when there is not a breath of wind, the sea is so still it seems to be sleeping, and the sun burns mercilessly down on all living creatures. There is no refreshment that satisfies, inside is hotter than outside, the water is like warm oil. He wanted a cold beer, and as he went in to get one he saw that a young woman was standing at the telephone and was dialling. She had her back to him.

He took his beer from the drinks cabinet, opened it, and leaned on the counter drinking, and as he did so began observing her.

The light was from behind, coming from the doorway and a small window next to it, so that although she was some five metres away, he could see her clearly.

They were alone together, since the proprietor was outside chatting loudly in broken English to members of the tourist group Andreas had brought to this little beach. He entertained them well, did Kostas, with his stories of fish and Greece. It let Andreas off the hook for a while.

He sipped his drink.

She looked very young, perhaps only eighteen. She had on a simple pair of shorts but these were of a very rich purple colour, were very tight fitting, and cut to the minimum. They showed off the small, neat roundness of her backside, and her strong, smooth legs. These ended in bare feet, one casually placed on top of the other, scratching it with the toes. It was an absent, yet somehow appealing gesture of youthful concentration. He also noticed with approval that her skin seemed silky and was tanned lightly brown.

He decided she must be attractive, although he couldn't remember having noticed her before. With forty people of mixed nationality to cope with, only the loudest, the most beautiful, or most difficult individuals came to his attention.

Then he noticed how the young woman's posture accentuated the special way her thick, naturally blonde hair, the colour of straw, had been cut into a short bob with thick, short bangs on either side of a central parting. It had been done so precisely that the hair-ends made a neat line which started on one side where it hung forward of her chin, swooped to halfway up her ears, then amazingly, climbed further up, high onto the back of her head, before swooping down again on the other side in perfect symmetry. The hair on the lower part of the back of her head and neck had been closely cropped to a little golden lawn that ended in a little point on her nape. This part of her head was now presented to him as she bent her head a little more. It was curiously vulnerable, this exposed neck, a kind of surrender and an invitation to whatever man might receive its message and accept it. In its shape, possibly, it imitated the newly grown lawn between her legs. Would this hair, too, he wondered, also come to a point just below the crotch? It might be amusing to find out.

Now she was speaking. It was in German and she had to shout.

'Hi Mum! It's Sonia! Yes! Ring back!'

Bad line. Sonia, he mused. Sonia. He liked it. Had she realised, he asked himself, exactly what she was doing, when she'd selected those shorts? Did she know about the small roundness of her bum? Did she know about the smooth power of her legs? Did she know about the tantalising line and colour and thickness of her hair? Did she know about the point on the back of her neck? Had she said to herself that she simply wanted to be cool for the summer, or had she been more calculating about her appearance and said I want to be erotic, sensual and inviting, turn men on, somehow tell them I'm ready now, ready for sex in the erotic heat, scents and sights of Greece, ready for experience, ready to learn about the delight and joy and pain of sex?

Suddenly he realised that the telephone was down and she'd turned and was looking at him. She was smiling and tentatively meeting his gaze. And he realised that he, too, had been smiling, and that the smile was the special one, the lazy one, which betrays desire.

This was a mistake. He'd been careless, and he needed to watch it, bring this tendency under control. His new rule was to show no interest in a woman whatsoever. He could be polite and friendly of course, but there should always to be that reserve. Just because he was a skilful seducer did not mean that he had to carry on seducing anything that was female and moved. He wanted to be more selective. From now on he would only let a woman know he'd noticed her, *noticed* her, her eroticism, her beauty, if there was something special about her and he really wanted her. And then it would be just this same smile - clear, precise, full of desire, unflinching - telling her that in that moment she was special, there was no one else, there never ever would be anyone else, only her until the day he died, she, she, was supreme above all other women, she was the one who had finally got him to surrender. Each time he almost believed it himself - until the next one, of course.

And now here he was smiling at a young girl with a funny little tail.

He didn't remove his gaze, however, but continued looking, drinking her in, admiring. Why? He didn't know.

She became a little embarrassed and spoke in English.

'My mother will call in a minute. Do you want to use the telephone?'

'It's OK. I can wait.'

'Thankyou.'

'I was admiring you,' he said. 'You're beautiful.' He was totally honest and sincere about this. She was beautiful, just as all the others were, too.

Now she was speechless, reddening slightly, but continuing to hold his eyes, the smile broadening into embarrassed surprise - pleasure, too.

But once again it had slipped out. He had been going through the motions. Next she would draw the conclusion that he had selected her, and yes that's what he was doing, he realised, selecting her, out of all the other attractive, perhaps more experienced young women, on the trip. For now. If it was one of those special days, those days that might happen once or twice a summer, then there would be more than one - two, or even three. On one memorable day the year before last he'd had five. By some miracle, although they had all been on the same trip, not one of them was aware of what was going on with the others, and he had taken each one differently: with one it had been oral, with another from the rear, with another from the front, and so on. And he could have had more, there were women waiting, but he'd run out of time. He'd had the last one as they were pulling into harbour, was just finishing as they reached the quay, and had to leap up, hurriedly fastening his trousers, to do the ropes. Fortunately it had got dark and they were all so drunk no one noticed. Oh, how the lads had laughed over that, till the tears came, and still did on occasions, in the bar, over ouzos.

Among Greek youth he hadn't been considered particularly attractive. This was because just about everyone was beautiful: beauty is commonplace in Greece. There was nothing special about him at all. In fact, if anything, he was considered a bit ugly because of how dark he was. This was associated with poverty and a peasant past. Everyone did their best to look like Northern Europeans now. They wanted to look like these fair, healthy, immoral, and very sexy invaders who'd started coming to his island every summer since he was a small boy.

The Northern European women never ceased to amaze him with their willingness to believe almost any flattery in their desperation for him to make kamaki to them.

Now in his late twenties he had got used to them. They were part of his life - no that's wrong, he thought, they *were* his life. And the island had needed them. But now they had comparative wealth, whereas before all there was was poverty and hard work. As a boy his job, when he wasn't in school, was to help his father on the *kaiki* get in the fish: dangerous and backbreaking work at times. But he was strong and able, and also clever. He was good at English at school and had picked up smatterings, enough to get by, in nearly all the other European languages just from sitting on the quay talking to the tourists, joking with them, playing with their children. Even as a child he'd seen that he must do this if he was to get rich like these people, some with yachts as big as the weekly ferry.

At fifteen, a tour operator, known to his father, and a distant relation, had asked for his help with day trips. From this small beginning, he'd worked hard, learned the business, and now, though not a partner, was very much a trusted accomplice in charge of the branch of the business that had to do with the sea: day trips, water skiing, pedalloes and so on. Some day *he* would be able to have a yacht as big as a ferry. This was his ambition, some way off yet, but he did already have a very nice little fishing boat of his own as well as being able to use the company's boats any time he wanted.

'You like the trip?'

She smiled.

'Oh yes, very nice.'

'I have something very special for you later.'

'Yes?'

'Sea cave. Very lovely. Not every group goes. For one thing the weather must be exactly right: completely calm, like today. But also there must be the beautiful woman. So today, especially for you, we go.'

He could see how much she wanted to believe it was true. A Greek woman would tell him to get lost.

'Thankyou.'

As on his very first trip with the American lady, this young woman had probably been looking at him, assessing him, from the moment they had set off from the quay in the gaily painted *kaiki* . It was his moment to shine, so he always got up and made a little speech with jokes in various languages, explaining about all the beautiful things they would see and how much they were going to enjoy themselves.

She'd already decided, perhaps, again like the American lady, that she liked this young Greek, with his slightly gawky, shy manner, subtly excusing himself for being there, his classic almost god-like dark looks, his black hair worn long, falling in natural ringlets about his face and onto his shoulders, his slim tanned body. At that time, of course, he was natural and naive. Now, he was the same, but it was carefully calculated. She would probably have dreamt a little bit of romance, without ever assuming, hoping even, that it would actually happen.

Then the telephone rang and she turned quickly and lifted it. She was speaking in German again.

'Mother? ...'

Now he was presented again with the strong, tanned legs, the small *poppó* encased in those brief, velvet shorts, the elegant back with its white T shirt, and above all the golden lawn on her neck.

He moved slowly towards her, putting his beer down on the counter as he passed. He took up a position very close to her, almost touching, leaning on the wall next to her as she spoke. He stared intimately at all the details now: a mole on the side of her neck, the down on her forearm, loving it all, and drinking in her delicate perfume.

'... Great time ... Hot...'

As she said this she looked up into his face and gave him quick smile, before turning away to concentrate on her call.

He realised that there was nothing specially beautiful about her. From the front her face was a face, nothing wrong with it. Her breasts were there, yes, like any normal young woman's, but no one would bring them up as a talking point at the end of the day when all the young men got together to swap yarns. Her legs were strong, but he preferred longer. Legs! It was a pair of legs that had been his undoing last week! There was this young girl, who could only have been about sixteen, who'd arrived with her family in a yacht. She'd had the longest legs he'd ever seen on a woman. And she knew it, too - so young and she knew it! She had these black fishnet tights with a strikingly bold flower pattern all over them which she put on in the evening, together with the shortest dress you could imagine, ending just below her crotch, and flaunted herself up and down the promenade. The family, who seemed very nice and well-to-do, and came from Denmark, appeared to tolerate this behaviour and took no notice of it. He'd given her the usual look, sitting outside the office (it was his duty night) and she'd responded. They'd had a chat full of compliments, and this had quickly progressed to touches. Then he'd invited her in for an ouzo, and in the office with the door locked and the blind drawn the touches had progressed to passionate kisses, and to feeling and stroking those gorgeous legs. Finally he'd felt her sex and found it so wet, and her so eager, he'd taken her there and then, quickly, from the rear with her over the desk with her tights and panties pulled down just far enough for him to get it in. It had taken him five minutes. Afterwards, she'd kissed him sweetly on the cheek and left. Next day the yacht had gone, and he was just going to mention to Stavros about his adventure when he had come out with the self same story: how he'd seen this girl with the long legs and tights off one of the yachts, given her the eye and then made love to her. And then Manolis, fat, hairy Manolis!. It turned out she'd copulated her way along the promenade. What seemed such a moist and lovely orifice was in fact other men's semen dribbling out.

He'd felt so disgusted that he hadn't dared say he'd had her too: just that he was busy with day trip bookings that night and must have missed her.

And he hadn't even bothered to use a condom! She was so innocent it hadn't seemed necessary. Then it turned out she was worse than he was! He'd had five one after another, but what about her? Was she even now boasting about how she had seduced so many, and how easy they were, back there in the stupid little port they'd just left? Maybe she had AIDS and was trying to get back at men.

He had been used. Utterly used.

Normally he would have felt nothing, but now he had been surprised to find that he did feel something: anger, degradation, fear of having caught something, but also, he didn't know what - a yearning - at least to know her name, for God's sake! There was no doubt about it, her behaviour had shocked him. It was so much like a mirror of his own and yet it shocked him. He'd been off women for the last week. He hadn't had one since, and this was very unusual for him. There had been opportunities, but he'd stopped himself and left them for his mates.

Yet, now, here he was, with another young woman, and after only a week's abstinence. If he wasn't careful he would drift into yet another meaningless coupling. Yes! That was it! He was after something to give it meaning!

And for all her averageness, there was something about her. Somehow there was a beauty within. OK maybe she was aware of her attractions. But she wasn't packaged and painted for desire, like so many. She was natural. In the past he'd been too easily hooked by a dyed head, a short dress, a pair of bright lips. It was all crass stuff, and the women were on holiday and just out for a bit of fun.

In his mind he'd been using them, exploiting them for his pleasure. But now it occurred to him that maybe it was actually the other way round. In many ways, he was beginning to think, he was the one who'd been used.

Ever since that first time on that first trip, when that American lady, who he'd always thought of as so beautiful, so rich, had taken such an interest in him, tousled his hair, taken him to her villa and there fondled and fucked him, who had done the exploiting, he or she? And so it had gone on, on all of those first trips in that first season, him passively being seduced, sometimes, looking back, by utterly repulsive women, although others had been young and very beautiful. Like the two Italians three years ago. Or was it four? Or even five? He'd lost count. One so beautiful the other so ugly. Spent all day in the boat, drinking, chatting him up. Then when they returned he'd spent all evening in the bar with them, finally suggesting his room to the beautiful blonde. But she'd refused.

'Not without fixing up my friend.'

So he'd called out Stavros, but he'd refused: the ugly one, no - just too ugly. He'd called a few other friends, and they'd dropped by to have a look. They couldn't do it. Not even ugly Manolis would do it. So he'd done the only thing left open to him: had them both.

Yes, all the woman he'd had! They'd only to touch his penis and it had spouted its milk, so it hardly mattered what they looked like, and he'd felt such a big man, too. And then he'd widened his horizons beyond the day trips to anyone on the beach or walking the prom who took his fancy: since they all seemed to fancy him, there was no problem.

Then it had become a game between him and his mates: scanning the beaches and making bizarre, impossible selections and laying bets on who could seduce her first. On one memorable occasion, they'd spotted this gorgeous blonde, dressed in shiny, kinky leather, with a fat slob of a man, old enough to be her father, and laid a bet on who could have her first. Desperate to get one over on Stavros he'd swum out to the couple's yacht as soon as it got dark, climbed on board, and peered in through the window. What he saw was a shock, and strangely fascinating. There she was, naked, strapped across a table, being whipped across the buttocks by her lord and master with a riding switch. When the whipping was over, without looking at her at all, he'd come up on deck, got in the launch, and headed for the nearest bar on shore.

Andreas had seen his opportunity, and gone down below. There she was, still strapped over the table. She'd looked up when he'd come in.

'You can fuck me. But whip me first. Please,' she'd said.

But he hadn't had the heart to do it. He'd given her a half-hearted thwang, done the business, and left. Back at the bar, Manolis couldn't believe it, so, as her partner was still drinking, he'd swum out, too. But he hadn't been nearly so churlish about the whipping - he'd given her a sound beating, satisfied himself, then stood in front of her and urinated right over her forehead. It had run down her nose, across her mouth, where she'd tried to drink it, but missed most of it and the pee had run uselessly down her chin onto the floor: his calling card. They were looking forward to nightly jaunts out to the yacht, possibly with parties as big as twelve, but the couple had slunk quietly out of the harbour early the next morning.

Wow! What a history...

And then there had been that German schoolmistress - how long ago was that now? She was one of Stavros's conquests. She had a mountain of brilliant red hair that tumbled down from her head like a shower of copper rain. Stavros had got off with her partly to find out if her pubic hair was the same colour, which it was, but had been amazed to discover that she had a pure white body - no matter how long she stayed in the sun she never changed colour: just stayed pure white, like Aphrodite. And what a body - perfect in every detail. Stavros had carried out the usual procedure with these uptight intellectual women, which was to take them out the first night, and be a perfect gentleman, not touch her at all. On the second night they were usually so desperate you had to hold them off. It had all gone perfectly to plan, he'd laid her, and the next day had brought her down to the beach to show her off to Andreas and Manolis, who, because of his hairiness and generally ugly looks had very little success with the girls. They were all naked, in a secluded spot they knew, among rocks. They chatted and drank beers. Stavros and the young woman had got to kissing, and then making love. Andreas and Manolis had watched the performance, getting more and more frustrated. When they had finished, Andreas had asked Stavros if he could have her, too, and Stavros had put it to her.

'This is my friend Andreas. He is like a brother to me. Whatever I have is his. Whatever he has is mine. So it is. I cannot refuse him. And he is a nice guy. Is he not a nice guy?'

'Yes, oh yes.'

'He thinks you are beautiful and desires you so much. I only ask this of you because he is special and you are special.'

'Anything. What is it?'

It was clear she was falling for it.

'Would you be prepared to let him make love to you?'

She agreed, so they'd changed places and Andreas had had her, too. Manolis had then taken his turn automatically without saying a word. He had simply got on top of her and she accepted him. Later, after swims, and more beer, they had all got randy again, she had started kissing all of them, and it had progressed to group sex. They all had her at once, one in each orifice. And she had squealed with pleasure - as much as she could with a full mouth, that is. Afterwards, they'd all felt rather embarrassed, and the party had broken up.

That evening it had all gone a bit sour, because she had been heard sobbing and loudly complaining to her companions that she'd been raped by three Greeks on the beach.

'Animals, just animals - no trace of civilisation.'

Stavros, who'd just been about to approach to say hello and how about the disco tonight, had crept away. Fortunately, she'd left soon after, but they'd had to lay low for a few days so as not to be spotted, and possibly pointed out.

What a history, and there was more, much more.

Back in the bar, standing next to the girl, he slowly raised his hand to the lawn at the back of her head, and gently stroked it. The little hairs felt stiff and springy, and resisted his fingers in the most delightful way.

He noticed the little shocks that ran through her body as he stroked her. She had to force herself to be natural and an edge came into her voice.

'Yes mother, yes of course, mother. Bye.'

The phone was down but she didn't move except to lower her head a little further so as to rest it on the receiver.

He began to massage deeper, more confidently allowing his hand to stray down along her shoulders and then up again.

She let out a little whimper, and he found himself kissing her neck now, using his tongue to get the texture and flavour of each crisp little golden hair, while the hand travelled down her back and he was using it now to massage the small round cheeks of her buttocks, the velvet of her shorts electrifying his fingers. He could hear more whimpers now, and her body began to move.

Shit! He was doing it again! Would nothing stop him? He didn't want to be her bit of holiday fun, a conquest she boasted about when she got back home, but otherwise meaningless for her.

He broke away angrily, walked to the door and stood looking out for a moment. He found his cigarettes in the top pocket of his shirt, took one and lit it. After a few puffs he turned to look at the girl in the bar. She was leaning with her back against the wall, eyes closed, breathing heavily. She must be wondering what had happened to her and perhaps even why the sensation of pleasure had stopped so suddenly. Now she was slowly calming down, her aroused body easing back to normal: good - she'll be all right, he thought.

He wanted to do it differently now, move on from all of that. Where was it taking him? Here he was, twenty-eight already. Give him another ten years and then what? There must be more to life than a long series of orgasms followed by death. But how *was* he to do it differently? If he asked himself, not what was the thing to do to get the girl, but what do I, in my heart of hearts, *want* to do? He didn't know. Instead, he acted mechanically.

He'd had women before in this bar many times. The last was only a few weeks ago with this fat Australian woman, a member of a group like this. She'd been eyeing him from the moment they'd set out. Why had he been attracted to her? She must have been fifty if she was a day. But when you've had as many women as he had, you begin to seek variation. There'd been a twinkle in her eye, a frankness in her lust that had appealed to him. She was jolly, too, spoke frankly, and enjoyed life, he could see that. She had come up to him offering drinks, being friendly, but above all just letting him know how much she appreciated him, and she'd won him over: he'd let her touch him and he'd started to touch back, but discreetly, so the others wouldn't know. He'd admired the way she'd managed this. Obviously she was a woman of understanding, she knew the ways of the world. Slowly a picture had formed in his mind of taking her, from the rear in the way he liked, that enormous arse raised to the winds, he grasping the blubber and ramming home. And the simple enjoyment of the two of them would be followed by no complications: not like taking a virgin when you had to practically promise marriage and then face the tears and fury afterwards, when you ignored her. No, this would be easy: they'd wave at each other across the street after, and at the end of her stay, travelling back to Australia, she'd think back and have a soft spot for him. And so it had turned out: he'd received a nice little card from her only a couple of days ago with a reference to fun in Greece, and a possible return next year. Yes, this had been a first. He'd always ignored really fat people before. Strong, well built women he'd had and liked them, but fat, no. And it had been interesting: once you'd made up your mind to wallow in the fat and really enjoy it, it had its own appeal. The group had come here as always, he'd come inside for his beer, and when he'd turned round, there she was. He'd kissed her and taken her behind the bar and made love exactly as he'd pictured, from the rear. The only hitch hadn't really been a hitch at all. He'd just got well under way when he'd heard a gruff English voice above him.

'I say, excuse me.'

He'd screwed his head round to look up, and there was the jovial face of an old English colonel type, moustache and all, not showing a trace of embarrassment.

'Don't want to interrupt old boy but can you point me in the direction of the beer?'

He'd pointed towards the cold cabinet in the corner.

'Thankyou very much, sir. Carry on.'

And he had, he'd carried on. Just like that. And the delay had actually helped. instead of him coming quickly and her getting no satisfaction, she had been able to orgasm too. He knew, because of her stifled screams at the end. The incident with the colonel had generated another little friendship. Norman, that was the colonel's name, had been coming to the island for a week or so every year for years, but they'd never exchanged so much as a greeting. From then on, for the rest of his stay, as he passed the office or the boat moored at the quay, he would wave a cheery hand, and make a motion with his elbow indicating 'keep it up'. He'd wave back and laugh. On his last day they'd had an ouzo together.

Had that been the beginning, the real moment when he'd begun to change? Maybe. That had brought up another issue he'd never really thought about. At the end of their two weeks, few days, or even single night, they always left. Whenever you met someone nice they always told you they were leaving. While this was very convenient from one perspective, from another it was highly frustrating. There was no time for continuity. The people who stayed were the locals who were born on the island, and a sprinkling of the tourists who made a home here. But everyone was so busy making something out of the others there was no time for deep contacts - a gossip and a joke, yes, but nothing more.

That was it - he didn't feel understood or appreciated as a person.

And of course that was something to do with his culture. As a child he was just an extra mouth to feed, and then an extra pair of hands on the boat. No one had had the time to understand anyone. The first and only problem was to fill your belly. And that's how they'd carried on once the tourists arrived. Filling their bellies, even though, with the amount they'd earned, many of them could fill their bellies many times over for the rest of their lives without doing another stroke of work, ever. But they'd mindlessly carried on salting it away under the bed, or, later, in the bank. And it had been the same with him and women. He'd pursued them as if he was starving. But now he wasn't - he'd had his fill, and more. Now was the time for something else. OK, he could play women like they were a musical instrument and he was the master musician, but that didn't mean he had to play anything and everything that came along. Some tunes were better than others, and some were classical music - very special indeed. It was time now for the very special.

Back in the bar, Sonia had recovered now, and was looking at him curiously.

'Sorry.'

'That's OK. It was nice.'

He offered her a cigarette and she refused, shaking her head. He motioned towards the drinks cabinet and she went over and got one for herself, a Coke. He went back to his beer.

They stood there, a few metres apart, not saying anything, just thoughtfully sipping their drinks.

He wanted to get to know this young woman first, before he did anything. But what was there to know?

'You're German?'

'Yes.'

'Student.'

'Yes.'

Perhaps he could share something of himself.

'I'm a fisherman.'

'Yes.'

How awkward and stilted it all seemed. What had appealed to him about the fat woman, in the end, had been her friendliness. And Norman's. But how to get friendly? You needed something in common, so you could talk. All he knew about was the sea. Yes, that was it, the sea! That was what he was here for. They relied on his intimate knowledge of the sea. It could turn from peaceful to rough in a few moments. And if it came to it, he would know what to do. And it often had come to it. You had to respect the sea and know it's moods, know just how far you could go with it. He loved the sea. It had a purity about it, which in some way they were now abusing, not only with their shit, their piss and their garbage, but with these trips themselves, in their meaninglessness. Yet there were coves he knew where the water was still crystal clear, and the fish teamed in abundance.

'Would you like to go fishing with me?' he said.

It had come out shyly, almost as if he was fifteen again. He had never ever taken a woman fishing, not without some other motive. It was always to impress some painted tart in a mini dress, so he could have his way, as perfunctorily, brutally, as possible - humiliate her there in the bottom of the boat among the dirty oil rags and bits of rope, before dumping her back on the quayside, soiled goods in more than one manner of speaking. He had abused not only the sea, but his boat.

Now he just wanted to take a girl fishing - show her some things, that maybe she'd never seen before. Be there with her. Nothing else, just that. Create a moment valuable and meaningful between them. She must have caught the hesitancy and sincerity in his voice, because her face changed and became much more serious. Now she had to work out how the hunt had changed. The lion could have eaten her if he'd wanted, but he hadn't. He'd opened his mouth and let her go. Now he was offering something completely different. Did she want it? He could see her thinking it out, and was nervous.

'Nothing special. Just fishing. Make a picnic. Maybe tomorrow.'

'Can I bring my girl friend?'

'Sure. Why not? Bring her. No big deal.'

'OK'

Late that night, in bed, he knew he was in a different world now. If he wanted a proper relationship with a nice girl he was going to have to learn new skills entirely.

He was actually nervous about tomorrow.

5. Surrender

She was perhaps thirty-something, and was tall and slim. The face was angular, not really beautiful except for the eyes which were intense and startlingly brown. They contrasted sharply with her blonde hair which was firmly scraped back into a bun at the rear. She had an angular body, too, under a plain, long brown dress reaching almost to the floor, that came right up to her long neck where it ended in a tight collar. Her slim, elongated arms were left bare. She wore no decoration such as earrings or a necklace. Nothing, not even a bracelet. The effect, he had thought, when introduced briefly to her when he arrived, was severe and rather forbidding.

Later, during an animated and highly intellectual discussion with a professor of architecture, he had happened to glance up, and had caught his breath. She was some distance away and had turned to talk to someone. The dress, so plain and simple and modest at the front, from the rear was very different. There was the brown collar at the top but beneath it - nothing. It was backless: the whole of the rear was cut away revealing her naked all down her long slim back to beyond the waist, beyond even the hips. The whole of her backside as far as the top of the thighs was visible. Here at last a curtain of cloth came across. And another startling thing: on her back, stretching all the way from one shoulder to one cheek of her backside was a brilliantly coloured serpent tattoo. It's head, with angry eyes and darting forked tongue was uppermost, and its body looped in serpentine twirls down the long back, and the tail, with a humorous knot in it, sat cheekily on her rump.

She had noticed him looking at her, and had responded

with a glance and a smile, which he had returned. A little later, partly seeking relief from the professor, he had left the company for a moment and gone to the library, with the intention of checking a fact. Finding the relevant book, he was standing there in the soft lamplight with it open in front of him when to his surprise, glancing up, he saw that the snake-woman was in the room. She stood looking at him, a strange light in her eyes and a smile on her face. Slowly, so slowly, she began to dance for him, squirming her body and rotating her hips. It was a snake dance, and he was mesmerised by it. Her hands began caressing her body, slithering up and down it and as they did so, unhooked the dress. After only a few such movements, it slipped to the floor and she stepped out of it, naked. Still squirming her body and rotating her hips, still caressing herself with her hands, she advanced toward him...

There was a knock at the door and a cough.

He was disappointed. It was a fantasy that never failed to excite. The reality had been so different. He had been introduced to her, yes, and later chatted with her a little. She excited and stirred him: what sort of woman was she that would dare to go so far, would surrender to the erotic to such an extreme? And she had seen his interest (how could it be disguised?) and flirted a bit, clearly available to royal command, but, afraid of yet another scandal, needing to do the right thing, he had merely commented on the snake:

'Absolutely spiffing. Very daring. Love to talk, but must go.'

And he had moved on to the next guest.

How he wished, sometimes, he had thrown caution aside and done it. But if it had got out, what would people have said? Later it had turned out she was some kind of journalist, so it was a lucky escape. But he longed to surrender to his desires, even if it was just once. Well, why not? It couldn't be worse than it was now. But all his training was against it. The serpent was locked in and could only wriggle out occasionally, in secret, in the most distorted and tenuous ways. His sexuality had been sacrificed to the needs of the state. Or, perhaps, not even that. It had been sacrificed to the needs of the media.

The knock was repeated.

Slowly, he came back to the present. Things had gone silent at some time in the night, exactly when he wasn't sure, but it was apparent that they had arrived somewhere. He rolled over and pulled aside one of the curtains to his cabin porthole and looked out.

They were just outside a little bay, and there, glinting white in the morning sun, was a little waterfront with a few bars and restaurants, with behind green forest, giving way quickly to high, rocky cliffs. To the right, one arm of the semicircle of beach became a quay where a few yachts were tied up. To his left, on the other side, rose a massive cliff of brown rock, and high, high up above it the outline of a castle. The water in the bay looked smooth and blue and inviting. He knew where he was immediately, since it was a view that was familiar to him. He came back here, to the island, every year at some point during his summer Mediterranean cruise.

He would have been happy to quietly contemplate the view for a few moments but it was abruptly blotted out by a dark grey mass.

'Damn!'

It was the warship. Ever since there had been threats on his life by a variety of maniacs it had been like this. Everywhere his yacht went it was shadowed by a destroyer stuffed with every conceivable weapon. It was now standing between his yacht and the coast, as it always did, supposedly to protect him, but in reality creating a prison from which, for the foreseeable future, there seemed little escape.

Animal rights campaigners wanted to kill him because of something he had said, in all innocence, about animals, sports fans wanted to kill him for what he had said about sport, artists and architects wanted to kill him for what he had said about art and architecture, nationalists wanted to kill him in a variety of regions and states for what he had said about nationality. And so on. Everyone wanted to kill him.

Why couldn't people see him for what he was? A bloke. An ordinary bloke just like them, neither better nor worse. A bit thicker, probably, than average. He ate like them, he drank like them, he shat like them. He even desired women like them. But they just wouldn't. And now the latest. He had done it with the best of intentions, admitting to an extra-marital affair in a TV interview. He had wanted to show how human he was. He was instantly branded an adulterer, and now there were guardians of public morals who wanted to kill him. There was no doubt about it, he had a habit of blundering into things. But there didn't seem to be anything he could do about it.

Even his retreat to this yacht was seen as a blunder. His very silence was seen as proof of cowardice - yet another reason for his execution. Dear, dear. What a world. He had even, in a weak moment, contemplated suicide, but that would be no good. He would simply be consigning his son to the same fate sooner than he had the right to expect. No, better to soldier on, do his bit as he saw fit, and take the flak. No doubt someone would eventually break through the security screen and put an end to his suffering. Then he would be seen as a martyr, but too late to benefit. Fortunately, probably, since even his martyrdom would be turned into a media fiasco.

The knock again.

'Your highness, early breakfast as requested.'

'Come in, Maitland.'

Maitland came in with breakfast. Maitland was his personal servant and bodyguard and looked very trim in white shirt and shorts. Maitland always looked startlingly trim.

'Breakfast, sir. We are at anchor. I notice, sir, that you have your designer stubble. Shall I have the motorbike sent ashore and lay out the appropriate things?

'Yes please, Maitland.'

'It is my duty to remind you that your security staff are very much against your going ashore, even on the most remote of islands. They are very concerned for your safety.'

He liked Maitland's formality and apparent neutrality. He didn't like being mothered. It reminded him of some of his nannies as a child. Once they started to mother you they got insufferable and they usually had to go. He realised that he knew very little about Maitland, although Maitland probably knew everything about him. He had been his personal servant now for about two years, succeeding to the post after his long-serving predecessor had decided to take the money and disclose all to the papers about his marriage. So far Maitland had proved to be entirely trustworthy and discreet. He had once idly questioned him about his private life:

'Is there someone waiting at home?'

'The lady wife, sir.'

'She can't see much of you'

'I serve, sir, she knows that. And she is well occupied with the boarding house and the daughter.'

'She sounds a capable woman.'

'Indeed, sir.'

On another occasion he asked Maitland about love.

‘Have you ever been in love, Maitland?’

‘Yes sir, as indeed you have, sir, I’m sure.’

‘And how was that?’

‘A disaster, sir. I now have a lady wife and daughter to support.’

That was all he knew about Maitland. He realised that the other relationships in his life were on much the same level. Snatched between more formal exchanges. Like the relationships a prisoner had with his guards. Oh for someone to talk to intimately, without pretence. But there just didn’t seem to be anybody.

Later, sitting cross-legged in meditation on the lonely hillside looking out to sea from high up, around him ancient remains, he breathed in the gorgeously scented air and slowly relaxed. There was an atmosphere here which seemed to get to the very heart of things. Was it the spirit of Aphrodite? It should be, since this was her temple, and the locals certainly thought that she had left something of herself behind. The ancients believed that you must always surrender yourself to the power of Aphrodite - in effect, to the life force. She was at the centre of all things. Jason had poured libations to the goddess before setting off in search of the Golden Fleece. Theseus had done so before slaying the Minotaur. And he was aware of other, terrible stories of those who refused to acknowledge her power in their lives, or tried to resist her. And he realised, too, that he was one of these. But what could he do about it? He had spent too long trying to suppress his spontaneity and his natural longings to change now.

In front of him was a cup of wine. He leant forward and picked it up, then held it aloft in offering, before slowly tilting it further and further to one side, until the dark liquid spilled out and splashed onto the earth.

He was interrupted by a good-natured laugh and an earthy, no-nonsense voice.

'Don't do that. It's a waste. Let me have it.'

It was a young woman. She was standing a little distance to his right. How long she had been there he didn't know, but clearly she had been watching the show. She was wearing army surplus gear: long trousers, a shirt, and rumpled hat, all in camouflage green and khaki, and on her feet were large Doctor Marten's boots.

'I was meditating.'

'Well, I could see you were in a world of your own.'

'Beautiful here.'

'Sorry if I've disturbed you but I was walking on the hillside and you passed me on your bike. I realised you must be going somewhere so I followed you.'

He liked her directness. He noticed that she had a gaunt look, the sort of face he'd seen in his visits to deprived areas. She was clearly used to work. There were straggles of sweaty fair hair sticking to her face. She was not a beauty. It was an ordinary face.

'Aphrodite's Temple. Been lost for centuries. I discovered it by accident a few years ago. Now, well, it's nothing, just a couple of Doric columns and some piles of stone. From the sea it passes for a piece of hillside. From the land, invisible. In classical times this was one of the holiest places in all of Greece. People worshipped the goddess of love here. And that's what the wine was for - not worship exactly, more a kind of acknowledgement, a libation.'

'Well, sorry, but I'm not Aphrodite. Cigarette?'

'No thanks.'

She took out a tin box, opened it, and began the ritual of laying out paper, inserting tobacco, and rolling it.

'It's killing me, but I must have my drug. So, you're an educated upper class sort of type.'

'Yes, that's true.'

'On holiday?'

'Trying to get away from it all.'

'Same here. Two screaming brats at home, if you'll excuse my language. No time for Aphrodite in all of that, I can tell you. But mind you, I love the kids. Wouldn't be rid of them for the world, if you know what I mean.' She lighted up. He realised she was studying him.

'Don't I know you?'

'It's not likely.'

'But there's something familiar about you, like I've seen your picture or something. Take that scarf off.'

He always wore a red scarf when travelling incognito on the bike because it covered his ears. Once you combined the ears with the long mournful face there was no mistaking him. It was characteristic and instantly recognisable. He removed the scarf.

'Oh my God. You're not -.'

'I'm afraid so.'

'Well. Would you believe it? I can tell my friends I offered you cigarette.'

'It was very nice of you. Thankyou.'

'You know something? I've always had a soft spot for you, despite what they say about you - but don't tell anyone will you?'

He shouldn't do it, he knew, but there was something about her so he did it anyway.

'Listen, er, I brought some lunch. I don't know if you fancy sharing it with me, but we are both here, it's a beautiful place, and it's lunchtime.'

She looked at him for a moment.

'You mean. With you?'

'Yes.'

‘OK. Never look a gift-horse in the mouth, that’s my motto.’

So they had lunch together, sitting side-by-side on the edge of a rock, she sharing her peach and bread, he opening the box on the rear of his bike and bringing out a feast complete with the rest of the wine. He didn’t know what it was, whether it was the wine, or the situation, or something about her, but he found himself telling her about his wish to do things right, be a real prince for his subjects, but how it all seemed to go wrong and as a result everyone wanted to kill him.

He found she understood, because she could apply it to herself.

‘I’m the same. I was great at school, could have got qualifications, but somehow I rubbed the teachers up the wrong way. They expelled me in the end. Then I got pregnant and my dad wanted to kill me. Had to leave home. Got a good job but I lost it. Know why? I worked too hard. They wanted to kill me because I showed them up. I was married but it didn’t work. Big mistake. He was an ugly brute but I didn’t know any better. Had to go to the women’s refuge. He was howling outside, baying for my blood. I was on the game for a while. Had to, to make ends meet. But wouldn’t do the kinky stuff and got beat up. Now I’m on the social, but you can’t live on it. Can’t enjoy yourself or anything. My friend Louise is paying for this holiday. She’d have come herself, booked it and all, but she can’t get away.

‘You couldn’t afford to pay for yourself?’

‘On social security? You must be joking. But mustn’t let them know I’m here or they’ ll want to kill me. Holidays aren’t allowed.’

‘And the kids?’

‘My mum’s looking after them. She’s a brick, my mum.’

They were mates. It was just natural. The lowliest meets the highest in a strange kinship. And so they passed the afternoon, talking and getting a little bit drunk on the wine. Both were prisoners on parole, if only for a time. And time was going by.

He was serious.

'Thanks for the afternoon. I've enjoyed it. I want to offer you something in exchange. Listen. Indulge me. I like to use my money in creative ways. If I could offer you something, one thing that would help you at this moment, what would it be?'

'Oh, just a miracle. I feel like Cinderella sometimes. Make me different for a night. Let me come to the ball, be a princess for once.'

He was amused. She could have asked for much more. He chose to grant her wish because it sounded fun and he needed more of that commodity.

'OK. I will fly in a famous makeover artist at my own expense. I know just the guy, who will for one whole day, cosset, caress, prepare, and transform. Then tomorrow evening we will have dinner. How about it?'

'OK'

He was up, immediately, impatient to be off.

'I must go. I'll give you a lift down.'

He packed up quickly, put on his head scarf, got on the bike and waited. He saw that she hesitated.

'It's a long way down the hill, and it's late.'

'I know it sounds stupid, but what will people say when they see me on the back of your bike?'

'Nobody knows who I am. I'm in disguise.'

'But I don't want you to get into trouble because of me.'

She was standing by the bike with such a worried look on her face that he was consumed with compassion. It seemed slightly ridiculous, yet it touched him, and did something to him deep down. Suddenly he had an affection for her and he could see that, in this slight figure, with all its courage and simplicity, there was also a kind of beauty.

'Trust me.'

'Yes, but can I?'

'I'm a very good driver.'

She was still hesitating. He decided to be tough.

'If you don't get on now I'll go. You have a choice.'

She got on behind him. She was so nervous she couldn't find where to put her feet so he guided them with his hands.

'Here and here. Now put your arms round me and relax.'

Two very tentative, surprisingly slight hands came round his middle. He set off as gently as he could. He could feel her tenseness and as the bike turned a sharp corner, she tried to steady herself by leaning the wrong way.

He stopped the bike.

'You must relax and cuddle me close. And when I lean you must lean with me. If you don't you'll kill us both. Open your eyes and look at me.'

She looked.

Why hadn't he noticed it before? The eyes were chestnut brown and rather startling.

'Your problem is that you are too stiff. Relax, and you will enjoy it.'

They set off again. He could sense her reluctance, but she did cuddle up, and as they progressed she got more relaxed, and he was able to take more risks, until finally the bike was leaping and bucking on the rough path, and both of them were moving with it, as if he, she and the bike were one, and it was a heady feeling. Then they were off the worst of the paths and had joined a dirt road and they could hurtle along at great speed, and they were laughing and joking about the fact that on one side was nothing, nothing at all for hundreds of metres, with way below tiny trees and a dry stream bed, and on the other side a sheer rock wall, jagged and terrible. If they went into either they would be annihilated, and it didn't seem such a bad prospect at that moment.

Then they were on asphalt and the bike was roaring along overtaking other vehicles, hooting. Then it was over all too soon.

'Here. Stop, please.'

He stopped the bike. They were outside the campsite. She got off.

He could see a few faces turn from the bar, which was just inside the entrance. He hoped she wouldn't have to make explanations.

They looked at each other in an embarrassed way for a moment.

'Come down to the quay at midday tomorrow. A boat will be there to meet you.'

He saw her hesitation again.

'Just like the motorbike. Let go. Allow it to happen. You only need to be you. If you get cold feet you don't have to turn up. OK?'

'No it's not about that. Can I ask you something?'

'Sure.'

'Suppose it was me driving the bike and you who had to get on the back, would you do it?'

It was a surprisingly challenging question.

'Ah. Of course there's the world of difference between driving a a bike and riding on the back. If you drive it your fate is in your own hands. If you ride on the back, you must surrender your fate to another.'

'That isn't what I asked.'

He looked at her. There was no escaping the truth.

'No I couldn't. I would have had to walk down.'

A smug smile crossed her face.

'I thought so.'

She walked away.

He was reading on deck when Alphonse emerged from his day-long session with her. He had changed for dinner and had realised half an hour ago that it was going to have to be a late one. The chef had been informed.

Alphonse was excited.

'I've done it. Amazing. How do you pick them?'

'I didn't. I think she picked me.'

'Anyway, it's sensational. She's going to be the next supermodel, I'm sure of it. I've offered to put her under contract - those legs!'

Yes he knew about the legs, long and powerful, always a weakness of his, legs, had realised that on reflection, but also the bashfulness that had emerged, this was another of his weaknesses. And the eyes. Yes, he had known in the end she was beautiful but didn't dare think about it.

He realised Alphonse was still babbling.

'I talked with her, we explored, it took hours but in the end she's taken the risk. You should have seen the scraggy hair, the army castoffs, the boots. And how gawky and unformed she was. But it was only when it was pointed out to me by my assistant that this was actually rather charming, kind of reminiscent of another famous person with whom your highness was once associated-'

The Prince's mind darkened slightly. He hated to be reminded of certain events from the past. Fortunately Alphonse was quick to recognise the signs and changed tack.

'I had to be so enthusiastic, so assured, kept coming back

to the same thing, convincing her, and for so long she wouldn't, but, well, in the end she did.'

'What made the difference?'

He smirked.

'That was very clever. The difference was in the word *and*. About being a princess *and* a working mum, going to the ball *and* having a job of work to do, moral *and* owning her immorality, being decent *and* showing her desirability, being discrete *and* outrageous, being her true self *and* playing a social role, indulging herself *and* caring for others - all at the same time. You see, she'd always put a but in somehow: like success but no fun instead success *and* fun. She was using buts all the time. A makeover, you must understand, isn't only in what you do to the subject on the outside. That's the minor part. Most of it is in the head. They must get the thinking right. Only then is transformation possible. Only then will they let go. Only then will they surrender.'

'Let's see it then.'

'You will. And you'll like it. It's so simple and startling, what I've done. The whole thing so false and yet in another way seeming totally natural, revealing something powerful, from the deepest recesses of her heart and her loins, beyond fantasy into the unconscious and out again. Revealed for who she truly is, a goddess. Actually it's an old idea of mine from way back, recreating it specially for her. Only an indication of course, to do the thing properly I'd have to take much more time and she would have to be prepared to suffer considerable pain.'

'Perhaps it would be best to just let me see her. I'm sure you've done a good job, you always do. How much?'

A shockingly high figure was mentioned, as expected, so, always aware that even a wealthy prince must bargain or he wouldn't stay wealthy, mentioned a much lower figure, and an agreement was made. Alphonse had a pressing engagement, a film star in desperate need of a breast lift, so was flown out immediately, much to his relief, not even staying for dinner.

He waited, only slightly curious, going back to his book.

It was some time before Maitland, unperturbed, showed her in.

He stared at her.

Nervously, she turned for him to see it all.

She was perhaps thirty-something, and was tall and slim. The face was angular, not really beautiful except for the eyes which were intense and startlingly brown. They contrasted sharply with her blonde hair which was firmly scraped back into a bun at the rear. She had an angular body, too, under a plain, long brown dress reaching almost to the floor, that came right up to her long neck where it ended in a tight collar. Her slim, elongated arms were left bare. She wore no decoration such as earrings or a necklace. Nothing, not even a bracelet. The dress, so plain and simple and modest at the front, from the rear was very different. There was the brown collar at the top but beneath it - nothing. It was backless: the whole of the rear was cut away revealing her naked all down her long slim back to beyond the waist, beyond even the hips. The whole of her backside as far as the top of the thighs was visible. Here at last a curtain of cloth came across. And another startling thing: on her back, stretching all the way from one shoulder to one cheek of her backside was a brilliantly coloured serpent tattoo. It's head, with angry eyes and darting forked tongue was uppermost, its body looping in serpentine twirls down the long back, and the tail, with a humorous knot in it, sat cheekily on her rump.

She stood looking at him, a strange light in her eyes and a smile on her face. Slowly, so slowly, she began to dance for him, squirming her body and rotating her hips. It was a snake dance, and he was mesmerised by it. Her hands began caressing her body, slithering up and down it and as they did so, unhooked the dress. After only a few such movements, it slipped to the floor and she stepped out of it, naked. Still squirming her body and rotating her hips, still caressing herself with her hands, she advanced toward him.

It excited and stirred him - what sort of woman was she that would dare to go so far, would surrender to the erotic to such an extreme?

Only, perhaps, Aphrodite herself. And she was asking him to surrender to her power.

'Ahem.'

It was Maitland.

'Yes, Maitland?'

'Dinner is served, sir.'

'Go away, Maitland. Please.'

'Yes sir.'

Maybe there was a way to surrender to Aphrodite *and* keep it out of the press...

6. Beauty and the Beast

Thirty is well known as a dangerous age for women. A woman of thirty is at the height of her sexual power and at the peak of her beauty. Yet it is at thirty that a woman is no longer able to kid herself she is young. The biological clock is ticking away and thirty is one tick too many. It is a dangerous combination and a woman of that age is capable of of almost anything.

It is no wonder, then, that a year ago, on her twenty-ninth birthday, Clarissa had said to herself that she would do it the instant she was thirty. Then it had been a way of putting the moment off - copping out yet again. But for a long time now there had been a growing sense of cheating on herself. There was something she needed to do. And there was a voice inside prompting her to do it, getting more and more insistent as every day passed. Here she was, not getting any younger, mouldering away in the library. She had to get out there and do something about her life. Not that she wasn't good at her job; she was efficient, and the customers liked her. One day, if she kept up the good work, she would have a library of her own.

For Clarissa it was very much about being what *she* wanted rather than what everyone else wanted, of expressing her deepest self. To do that she would have to cross a line of decency, of acceptability, put herself at risk. And if she didn't do it now, would she ever do it?

She had a partner, Brian, who she had met at university. He was an engineer, and their mutual lifestyle involved a heavy commitment to Morris Dancing, the men dancing while she watched with the other wives and girlfriends. This was supposed to be life. They weren't married, but were engaged and had been for ten years. Somehow neither wanted to tie the knot. They made love occasionally, but really were just good friends. She sensed if she left Brian he wouldn't really mind, so long as they could have chats now and then. And that was the core of it. She wanted more. There was a part of her that just wasn't prepared to stay unexpressed. It kept popping up and insisting on being noticed. It made her do the oddest things at certain moments.

Like when she was on the Internet for purely professional reasons, it made her go, despite all reason, and in the face of all her will, to that certain page. That page where they worshipped women like her, encouraged them, gloated over them. Bored with her work one day a couple of years back, and listening to that inner voice, she had typed it in, the name, stark and terrible, and found herself among friends. Not that the 'friends' knew about her. She was one of the millions of silent ones who visited and left without speaking.

Clarissa's birthday was in August. It was at five minutes before midnight four months later, on December the thirty-first, with clatter and clang of yet another Morris Dance in her ears and a pint of beer (Brian's, not hers) in her hand, that she realised time was passing. If she didn't make a move soon another year would have gone by and nothing would have been accomplished. In the moment the dance ceased, and the notes of 'Auld Lang Syne' began to ring out, she decided she would actually do it and nothing would stop her. And having settled that, the only problem was how to accomplish it.

She set about it methodically. Her first step was to break her silence on the Internet by announcing her intentions. There was such a chorus of warm support that she was encouraged to immediately put in for five weeks' special leave beginning just before her next birthday. She decided it would have to be in secret, alone, so no one knew, apart from her friends on the World Wide Web, to whom she was known only by her first name, anyway. A holiday on her own was the answer. And where else but on a Greek island? Where could be more anonymous, if you wanted to act out a fantasy?

Then she warned Brian of her intentions. Brian had been very understanding. Too much so. He fully understood she would want to be alone on her thirtieth birthday. He would go bird watching.

Before January was out she had booked tickets through the Internet, saying to herself that if she was a coward she didn't have to take them up. And she'd found just the island on the Internet, too, mentioned on a Greek page hardly anyone ever visited. It seemed the ideal place: quiet, idyllic, forgotten. A place to be your true self.

So here she was, it was August, it was her birthday, the flight and the ferry had all been perfect, she was thirty at last, she was alone in her own little holiday apartment, she was utterly private. Everything was prepared. All the tools she would need including multiplug adapter for foreign countries were set out before her. She only had to do it.

And what was the word she had typed into the computer so starkly?

'Bald'.

It had produced a screen so full of lascivious and pornographic references to that one word that she had immediately, in total confusion, abandoned her search, and gone back to her work. But later a refinement had popped into her head:

'Bald Woman'.

But this had produced another screen full of pornography, if somewhat more abated. Finally she tried.

'Bald Woman Admirer.'

That's what she wanted to be. A bald woman. And to be admired for it.

This had led to something more sensible, and by playing around a bit, in little moments over a few days, she soon got to a links page and before she knew it a message board just for people like her, and an even more special page called:

'The Bald Woman Admirers Society'

Oh, how she longed to be brave enough to be like the women pictured there!

She had once asked Brian what he thought, not directly, more a joke, after seeing a bald woman on TV, the sight of which never failed to excite her interest.

'Suppose I went bald.'

He carried on reading the paper.

'Do what you like.'

With Brian all she had to do was put on a pair of red suspenders and a pair of black stockings and he was away - premature ejaculation wasn't in it. He was in and out and finished before she'd even got started.

He seemed content, but she wasn't. It had to come off, this stuff on her head that she hadn't asked for, but insisted on growing at an alarming rate.

The best she'd done up to now, in the hairdresser's, was sitting there with the gown on, pressing the hairdresser sometimes to cut it a little shorter. But Mark, who knew her well, or thought he did, never listened much. He knew her style. About two inches on top - he would measure it with his fingers, getting its length.

'It will stand on end if it's any shorter.'

And that would never do for a librarian. A librarian couldn't be outrageous. You couldn't cross the line. You had a duty to the public to be boringly neutral.

She always loved it when a young woman came in with an outrageous style, like the other day, and dyed in all the colours of the rainbow. The assistants sniggered in the staff room but she defended her, saying it looked nice, and she had complimented the young woman, going out of her way to do so. And she was so nice about it, such a pleasant girl.

'I think you're so brave. I'd do it if I dared'

But she didn't dare. Not till now. Now she was going to. Sitting naked in front of the mirror, scissors in her hand, she looked at herself. Could she take it? Would she be ugly? She had a pleasant face with regular features and, she thought, a lovely smile. Her ears were small and clung to her head so wouldn't stick out. No, that was no reason to stop herself. The glasses of course had been ugly, but she had taken care of that on the first of February by going over to contact lenses. She'd found them uncomfortable in the past but had persevered this time and had in a very few weeks made the transition.

She liked her legs, which were long and slim. She was tall for a woman, and towered over some men. This was awkward at times but she quite liked being tall. Her breasts were nicely sized and not unshapely. Her skin was pale and didn't tan well, so she kept out of the sun. Pale was fine. What her looks needed and lacked was something dramatic to give them focus.

And now, at thirty, they were going to get it. Before she was too old. And it was going to happen now, this minute, here in Greece. The 'Bald is Beautiful' page on the Internet had given her all the instructions she needed for doing the job.

She put the scissors to her forehead like she'd seen pictures of naughty Suzy doing on the web and... snip. It was the first cut that was the difficult one. Right there in the middle, and a hunk of oh so sensible hair fell to the floor then another snip and another chunk and then snip, snip, snip and three more fell, and before long she was frantically snipping all over, guessing in the places she couldn't see, feeling for it with her fingers and then - snip!

Then out with the clipper, the little one that ran on batteries, just like Suzy used, having found one, would you believe it, in her local pharmacy.

And it was so easy. You switched it on and a high-pitched whine of pure cutting energy filled the room. Impulsively she passed the naked clipper's hot metal right down the centre of her head - zap! An inch-wide strip of white scalp appeared, and then zap again and it was like noughts and crosses. Oh Suzy, Suzy, just like you in those naughty nude photos doing it to yourself! What fun! No wonder you were smiling! And she zapped the rest, filling in the gaps and then went over it all again just to make sure. Then on impulse zapped the eyebrows, too, first one as a test, and looking bizarre with only one eyebrow, zapped the other. Zapped her pubic hair. It all had to go. Zapped her arms, zapped her legs.

But after, not really bald yet, not shiny bald, still the lightest of dark fuzzes.

So, gone too far to stop now, and trembling slightly, she set about the final step. In the anonymity of a large supermarket she had bought an expensive 'advanced technology' man's razor and a can of foam. And, in front of the mirror, did it. She sprayed the foam all over, making herself into her own iced birthday cake, and bit by bit did the whole body: scrape, then careful scrape. Legs. Thighs. More careful now, the pubes, carefully pulling the skin, and cleaning them with the razor then up over the belly, up over her breasts right up to the nipples, arms, armpits, then at last the head.

It was so easy and in the silence just the scrape, scrape of the razor and the smell of soap - total concentration. Difficult at the back. Matter of guesswork, but patience and peering into two mirrors after each trial did it. Then the eyebrows, carefully holding the skin taut with one hand and then going against the grain, scrap, scrape till there was nothing. Nothing at all. Skin. Pure, white skin. The eyelashes were the worst, plucking them one by one. Ouch! It brought tears to her eyes.

Afterwards, she walked around the room just being bald for herself for a while. Sometimes glancing in the mirror. And she was outrageously bald. Just eyes, the dome of the forehead. Nothing else. And beautiful. Stunningly beautiful. She was more beautiful than she had believed possible. It was a transformation. A tall, slim beauty had appeared.

Whenever she went on the Internet, first the modem dialled up and then, when it entered cyberspace, there'd be a rush of white noise and it went 'Gosh' to itself in the absolute amazed wonder of it. And that's how she went now, looking at herself in the mirror.

'Gosh.'

She'd entered cyberspace.

So it was with a little racing of the heart that she donned the special long white dress she had bought. She looked demure, wonderful, yet sophisticated and daring. She had certainly crossed the line now.

She went out. She looked neither left nor right. Just went. Yes, there were looks, sniggers even, but she paid no attention. Of course there were. You couldn't expect to walk about shiny bald without getting them. But it didn't matter. She went into a shop, chosen at random. It sold jewellery and she aimlessly placed herself in front of a rack, happy to be out of the sun, in a shady place, and alone for a moment among festoons of handbags and silk scarves. But she soon realised she wasn't alone. As she picked up a coloured glass pendant, blue like the sea, there was a voice.

'That is not for you.'

Involuntarily, she looked up. She locked on to a big brown eye, which didn't blink, just stared. She stared back in disbelief at a strange, Neandertal-like figure, which had just appeared in a doorway at the far end of the little shop.

What made the man so beast-like was his hairiness. Dressed in the shortest of denim shorts and one of those T shirts that are cut to the minimum, his forest of body hair was displayed to the full. He really was enormously hairy: hair sprouted from everywhere, black and abundant. Thick black hair poured from his head and fell on his shoulders in a tangled, greasy mass. On his forehead were two thick, overhanging black eyebrows which met in the middle. From his chin grew a thick black beard, so long that it merged with the dense undergrowth of hair on his chest. Hair sprouted from his shoulders in mounds. Tufts of it forced their way out from under his armpits. Hair tumbled down his forearms onto the backs of his hands, and down his legs onto the tops of his sandalled feet. She could imagine it growing like moss down his back and across his abdomen. On top of this, he was overweight and had an exceptionally short stature. To match was a squat face, and he was sweating. Rivers of it ran down his brow and disappeared into his beard. His T shirt was stained with vast patches of it. He was physically disgusting. There was no doubt about it - he was every woman's nightmare vision of a sex fiend.

Yet Clarissa liked what she saw. It was the exact opposite of her own lanky baldness, and thus accentuated and even complemented it. She felt superior, powerful and consummately beautiful before it. She could tell, as all women can tell instantly, in that special moment when two eyes meet in stunned lust for the first time, that he worshipped her and wanted her.

She was flattered and pleased. She relaxed, ready to taunt him lightly with her bald beauty, flirt with him even. She knew she could twist him round her little finger. He would do anything for her. And she knew all this in one single millisecond.

'Excuse me, but that is not for you.'

'Why not?'

'For yourself or someone else?'

'For myself.'

'If it was for someone else, OK, you can have it, who cares?' The accent was thickly Greek. 'But for you, no way. Not while Manolis is alive on this planet. Yes?'

She loved it. She drank it in. She wanted more. This was not Brian. This was something else entirely. This was what she had come for. True romance.

'What would suit me, then?'

He fished in his damp pocket and came up with a huge bunch of keys, from which he selected one, and advanced on a cabinet standing against the wall.

'For you, as for all beautiful woman only one thing is good enough. Gold. I decorate you in gold,' he said, 'Pure gold, nothing else - this and only this is what your beauty needs.'

She smiled.

'Expensive.'

'Of course.'

'Well, another time perhaps.'

'Wait.'

He struggled with the lock for a moment, the cabinet door swung open, he reached in and he turned to her triumphantly.

'Here. Take it.'

He was holding out a small, heart-shaped locket on a chain. It was made of gold.

She couldn't help tittering in English awkwardness and embarrassment at such grandiose and Mediterranean generosity. She was tempted. It was the first time in her life such gallantry had been shown to her. She only needed pressing.

'From the beast to the beauty.'

'But you're not -. I couldn't'

'Please. You are in Greece. Take it for me.'

She relented, and took it.

'How can I thank you?'

'Don't. To wear it is enough. May I?'

'Oh, but of course.'

He approached, and she bent her knees for him so she was more his height, and bent her bald head towards him. He raised the locket and slipped it over the head. She was not fooled when, in apparent clumsiness, he was unable not to allow himself the pleasure of 'accidentally' running his hands over the smooth skull as he slipped it on, and then stroking her smooth shoulders with his damp hands on the pretext of adjusting the way it hung, even putting the back of one hairy hand on her chest to hold up the locket once it was in place. Nor could he resist a final repulsive innuendo.

'It opens - see? You could put a picture of your lover's you-know-what in it.'

'My lover wouldn't be interested. It's not that kind of relationship.'

'I'm sorry. For a woman like you it should always be that kind of relationship. What else is good enough?'

He took the bony hands in his fat ones and guided her to a mirror. He stood behind her, allowing himself now to hold her by the smooth arms.

'There. That is beauty.'

They were both in the mirror: the smooth beauty and the hairy beast. Then a strange thing happened. On an impulse, the beauty twisted her long neck round, bent down, and pecked him on the cheek. Then she was gone, out of the door and into the street.

She had lunch at a shady taverna with a view out over the bay far below. The waiter had come to her first, ignoring others calling for attention, and had made her comfortable. It was a gallantry she was not used to, and she liked it. As she ate, her mind kept going back to events in the shop.

It had happened. A man had desired her. The man in the shop was passionate about her. She was sure of it. He had touched her in certain unmistakable ways, unable to resist her charms. Nevertheless, one shouldn't appear too keen. The kiss at the end, was that too much? He mustn't think her loose, an easy lay. Maybe she should make herself scarce for a while. Tomorrow she would find an excuse to go back to the shop - for earrings, perhaps.

So how was she to entertain herself this afternoon? She didn't fancy the beach. She wanted somewhere bucolic, peaceful. She took out the little local guidebook she had purchased on arrival and decided to visit a waterfall inland.

But how to get there? Taking her life in her hands, she decided to rent a little motorbike: if she went at a slow speed there would be no danger. The man with the motorbikes was over the moon at her request and assured her she would have no problem. Of course, she had the advantage of the very latest machine, snatched from the grasp of a less dramatic-looking young woman tourist, who, on the flimsiest of excuses, had to put up with a rusty old machine which rattled ominously and squirted clouds of blue smoke out the back.

So, after five minutes' intensive instruction, full of more 'accidental' and 'caring' touches and strokes, while the other tourist had to fend for herself, and looked on fuming, she wobbled off in search of the waterfall.

She wound her way through the narrow streets of the old town and then out into the country. It was her first venture into the Greek countryside and she found it wonderful. This was true cyberspace. There was beauty everywhere: high rocks adorned with thyme and sage, green forests of pine loud with cicadas, and above a blue, blue sky. Her soul soared.

Every so often she would pass an old man on a donkey or a woman in a field and shout 'waterfall' at them. In response she'd get the word *'Ekei'* and a pointed finger. It wasn't long before she arrived at a little village and just beyond it, casually on the side of the road, a primitive wooden notice with painted on it in English, with a shaky hand the word 'Waterfall'. An arrow pointed diagonally downwards. She realised she was going to have to walk down a cliff-side, but she parked the bike and did it. It was a ravine. Down and down the narrow path went, she tripping in her high heels on what were once possibly steps but now were little better than rocks, and as it went down the atmosphere got cooler and cooler. Eventually the sun was blotted out by trees.

Then suddenly there she was by a little stream and ahead of her she could hear rushing water. In a few moments, after walking in the direction of the sound, there in front of her was - the waterfall.

It spouted from a tangle of vegetation way above her head and plunged in a torrent fifty feet into a deep grey-blue pool. All around her was green vegetation, scented and dark, with gentle dapples of sunlight falling through the leaves.

She was utterly alone and at peace.

A phrase came to her as she stood there on the edge of the pool: Aphrodite's bath. That's what it was. It had to be. How could Aphrodite resist bathing in such a beautiful pool, washing her lovely smooth body in that refreshing cataract? A well-placed rock even made an ideal diving board. She stood on it, looking into the clear, pure water.

Come to think of it, how could *she* resist?

Why not? She was alone. It was private. She looked round, checking. The place was utterly deserted. She was alone in wild nature.

Impulsively she stripped off her dress, and naked, plunged in.

The water was clean, icy cold and wonderful. Laughing, she swam under the waterfall itself and abandoned herself to the sensuous feel of the water splashing her sensitive head.

Having enough of that game she decided to swim back to the rock and rest for a while.

She was just about to climb out onto it, when she became aware, as she had in the shop, that she wasn't alone. Some movement had occurred in the bushes. She peered into the gloom.

She could only see a vague shape.

'Who is it? Why don't you come out and show yourself? Don't you know it is rude to look at a lady while she is swimming?'

The figure emerged from the undergrowth and approached the edge of the pool. It was the beast! He must have followed her! In a panic, she swam back to deeper water and dived under. Coming up a moment later, she looked back. Now he was on the rock, looking in.

From the safety of distance she found that she was fascinated. Did she really have that effect on him? How wonderful. And what was he doing now? Holding something out, two things, one in each hand. Earrings! He'd thought of earrings! To go with the locket!

She laughed.

'Jump in. Come on! It's lovely!'

He understood and in a trice he was naked and he was in, laughing too, and they were playing games and he was splashing her and she him and then he was grabbing at her and she squealing and getting away, so lithe in the water, turning on him and pinching his bottom, and then he was kissing her, and she was wriggling out, and then she'd found, even in the cold water, she was knocking against a hard penis, and squealed even more and was making for the shore, but so was he, and she was out and the beast was lumbering after her as she flitted nude and shaved and white and slim and oh so bald through the trees and he was on her, and she could feel the prickle of his beastly black hairs against her skin, and she was on her back on a bed of dead leaves, and it was peaceful looking into his eyes.

She stroked his hair and his beard, and his hairy chest, and smiled.

Now he touched her, first on the buttocks, then up her front and over her breasts, then suddenly up to her neck and she gave a cry as his hand stroked her smooth scalp, marvelling in it. He was definitely a Bald Woman Admirer.

Then suddenly he was in her, and it was hard and big and pumping and she was coming oh so strongly, over and over, she couldn't believe it as he pumped and pumped, coming himself suddenly, briefly, beast-like, and rolling off.

And peace again as they lay there among the dry leaves in the cool shade.

And she wondered in that moment, who was the beast, he for what he had done, or she for luring him so blatantly?

And that was the beginning. And so far as I know the two are still together. Not on Aphrodite's island. The shop belonged to Manoli's mother, and now he had a woman she wanted him out. So they moved to another island. Where was it? Spetses maybe, or Santorini, or perhaps even Mykonos or Paros, I forget. But anyway, one of those more popular islands where the season is longer and you can make more money. And they set up a huge emporium selling everything you never thought of wanting till you walked in, including of course a line in expensive gold jewellery.

She never went back to dreary old England. She sent her resignation by E-mail. So if you ever go to Greece and walk into a shop festooned with tourist goods and you see there a woman, lean and cool and bald behind the cash register, and serving with her is this hairy monster who answers to the name of Manolis, and you see the tenderness between them, how he worships her and she, well, in a beastly way, clearly desires him, even after all this time, just think: maybe it's them. Buy them a drink and remind them of me - you know, the guy with the pen in his hand from way back. And if you don't travel in body, but in cyberspace, and you happen to come across a page devoted entirely to erotic pictures of hairy men with bald partners, which is only updated out of the tourist season, maybe it's them, too. Send them a cheery E-mail and remind them of me - you know, the guy with the pen in his hand from way back.

7. Marilyn

She watched him steer the little kaiki so that it nosed its way toward the shore, he guiding it as a man should, so safely and surely, while she decorated the deck with her beauty and allowed him to do it.

She desired him still , she reflected, even after so long. He looked like a legendary warrior standing there at the tiller, with his dark hair, so strong and naturally falling in curls, even though trimmed severely back these days, those beefy forearms covered with their rich forest, the naked brown chest, the strong chin with its carefully cultivated day-old bristles, the rich, dark brows. All this had attracted her so much on that first day when she had walked into his bar wanting a job. Even now, after ten years, they still attracted her. And so did his easy confidence, the know-it-all smile, his relaxed power with people and his pride. He was proud of everything, she reflected, proud even of himself, such a contrast to her with her doubts and fierce intellectuality. To him life was easy, with clear priorities, whereas to her it was a constant struggle.

He was concentrating on the task, aware of his skill, relishing and enjoying it, as they left the rough waves of the open sea whipped up by a strong breeze, and entered the smooth water between high, sheltering cliffs, knowing every centimetre of the channel below, heading for the tiny strip of beach at the far end of the inlet.

Then the boat hit smooth sand and he jumped ashore and made fast all in one movement. Then came back, wading, ready to lift her out as a man should, she behaving as a woman should and handing out the stuff and then teetering on the edge, inviting him to lift her, which he did, she squealing in appropriate style, he pretending to drop her, then the two of them still for a moment on the edge of the water, looking first at the narrow cleft between high rocks, then at the clean, white, fine sand - the colour of her hair.

Now he was looking at her, seeing the whiteness of the newly re-bleached head, white right down to the the roots and wanting her, suddenly. It pleased her to see it still had the same power over him, so she pouted at him, and he leaned forward for a kiss. But she decided to tantalise him and slapped him lightly across the face and squealed.

'Put me down you big idiot.'

The last word was in Swedish. She put more of her native tongue into her Greek than she needed to because she knew it amused him.

He chose his spot and put her down gently on the sand next to the things. She handed him the parasol and started laying out the stuff, so he shoved the end hard in and erected the shade, before stripping naked and plunging into the water for a first swim.

There was an intensity and concentration about his swimming that betrayed his frustration and showed how aware he was of her, the blonde on the beach. Arranging herself under the shade, she adopted the expression where it seemed she had been, perhaps, a long time on the streets, the prostitute, the sullen, used one, but the one with all the power really. The same as in the photos he'd taken of her was it five years ago? when she'd been so tired after a night's drinking but it could have been fucking for all the camera knew, kind of world-worn and cynical.

It had been so calculated, the bleaching. She had held it for so long this time, almost let her hair grow out. She had talked about it, said she might do it, just to wind him up. This was always her threat, to let it grow out, then without warning she had suddenly gone out and had it done yesterday morning, an expensive one with all the trimmings. And then holding him off in the siesta, insisting on a sleep before going out to serve in the bar.

It had been a long season of hard work, and the sex had somehow not happened this summer, not till this moment, with a bit of time to themselves at last.

Yes, and they had been together a long time. That's why she'd done it, for the anniversary. It was strange how they'd met. She remembered coming to the bar that first time, desperate for a job, and him absently saying 'come back as Marilyn Monroe' and turning away.

She simply wasn't there - strange feeling that - to be invisible to someone. Couldn't wait to get away to an Italian bitch. Bleached yes, but Marilyn? Ugly, couldn't he see that? And no spring chicken any more, either.

Ten years had left him a bit thinner on top perhaps, and a bit greyer maybe, he was thirty-six after all and she, let's face it, more than a bit thicker round the middle than before, too many moussakas, but still attractive for all that, still only twenty-nine, and not a spring chicken either, now.

She'd learned later that he'd just opened the bar. The premises had come up, the old man who ran it as a traditional *cafeneon* had died and the family didn't want to take it over; they had interests in Athens and basically wanted shot of an island bar, provided a good rent could be had.

He was fed up with his business renting motorbikes which had been very successful, but was hard work with the breakdowns, and a big servicing job in the winter. But he had put by a pot of money, so he sold the business to his arch-rival at the other end of the beach, more or less for a song, and set himself up as a high class bar owner, converting the premises over the whole of one winter, with the help of friends.

When June came he was ready and there was no other bar like it on the waterfront. This was up-market as only Athens knew, with the best inside decor, and waterside furniture with the Far East as its theme. Prices would be unbelievable. Only the rich from the yachts would call in, and young people wanting to make an impression.

He'd got to the point of looking for girls to serve: you had to have these because it attracted the men. But they had to be the right sort, not just any local peasant girl. You had to have the look: upmarket to match the prices, the glasses, the eatables. The exact image. That's what he wanted. He'd turned away so many.

'This isn't a bar for scruffs. You've got to look the part. Understand? Come back as Marilyn Monroe and I'll hire you'. Marilyn was his thing: was then, was now, always would be. One hell of a high class bitch. It was what he wanted.

Then the next day she'd walked in, straight from the hairdresser's. Marilyn Monroe. Despite all her principles she'd gone and done it, spent her last drachmas. And even then enjoyed the rejection of the natural for the totally false, having seen other women do it, and this falseness seeming suddenly so natural - after all hadn't human beings decorated themselves since time immemorial? So had her reasoning run to convince herself. But, in retrospect, she knew she would have done it anyway. There she was, so fresh on the island, fresh from Sweden, there for the summer, place booked at college to study of all things the environment. And she'd fancied the guy like crazy, and more in anger and sense of dare than anything else, just to prove anyone could, she'd done it. She'd so prided herself on being independent of men, but him not paying any attention had fired her up. And it came out so well. She hadn't known she suited it. She had only dressed in browns up till then, and used environmentally safe products, and then gone back on that completely and got bleached, got the dress, got the shoes.

'Hello Marilyn,' he'd said, sort of off-hand, as if Marilyn Monroe walked into his bar every day.

That was the image. Hair bleached white and done Marilyn style, wearing a dress like Marilyn's, red lipstick like Marilyn's, black high heels like Marilyn's, and of course you could see the bra jutting incongruously out, an enormous balcony at the front, even the beauty spot on the cheek, all just like Marilyn's.

He'd taken her on instantly. She'd asked for living accommodation and a wage as well as tips, but he desired her and he gave her everything she wanted.

She was an instant success. The men came and were touching her up all night. And she'd known her job, too. She let them get away with it, but not too far, buttered them up, drew out their drachmas along with their unrealised hopes.

Yes, she'd had it done, she was thinking. For him. Always against her better judgment, always with a struggle, with a fierce resentment, yet wanting to, wanting to be his object just as he was her object.

What was he doing out there in the water? Still pretending to ignore her. From out there he would be able to see her, the sexy bitch, not letting him have her yet, but he would get it in the end, he would know that. He would be annoyed by her effect on him, so he was staying in the water longer just to prove he could. Then she saw him turn and head for shore. Despite himself and his damn pride he was coming out. And when out, he stood there for a moment, dripping, looking back towards the sea, facing away, so she could see him and want him. Then flopped down beside her, spraying her with wet.

'Hey!'

Then he reached out and stroked it, the blonde hair, feeling its silky smoothness.

'Hey, you're messing it up.'

But she let him do it, showing no sign of affection, creaming up down there but not so as he would know. Now his fingers were following the way it was turned under at the ends, and she could sense the tremble in his hands as he did it, and she knew his penis would be stirring, the penis that would in the end overpower her, force her to bend to its upright will.

Then suddenly there were voices behind them and a crunching on the sand and she realised they weren't alone.

And past them came a young woman, with a beautifully slim and rounded brown body, and sprouting from her head a cascade of black corkscrews that tumbled down to her shoulders. She walked past them, naked, and plunged into the sea. It was clear that she must have clambered down the steep cliffs at the rear of the tiny bay. And after her, three others, two men and a woman, chattering in French and equally naked, plunged in, too. After swimming out to the entrance to the open sea, perhaps a distance of a hundred metres, Corkscrews splashed about a bit, and returned with a smart crawl to the shore, ignoring her friends. Then she emerged, proudly displaying a flat chest and a large, unruly triangle of black pubic hair between her legs. She didn't look once at the couple on the beach, just shook her head so the corkscrews freed themselves of the weight of water and bounced back up again, then walked quickly up the beach.

He had been looking at the young woman, and despite her knowing his preferences, she was jealous.

'You want her?' she asked, to test him.

'Of course I do.'

Her knowing this, knowing it was part of the endless game between them and not wanting to be drawn in really. Nevertheless she pursued it.

'Have her then. Why don't you?'

'Maybe I will.'

'You could go over now - chat her up, maybe she wants you.'

'Maybe she wants you.'

'You'd have her once just for the novelty, wouldn't you? And then she'd have to straighten it and bleach it, wouldn't she? Do you think she'd look nice bleached? Would she do it for you, do you think, like I do?'

'I'll find out if you like. She'll be at the bar tonight.'

But she knew he wouldn't. He was faithful, even though he was laughed at for it.

'Where's the wife, then?' his friends said.

They weren't married, just living together, but it was as if they were.

Then a look between them, her full of anger and jealousy and he, she could see, full of a double want, the both of them. Men were disgusting. But proud of him for it, too. This was a real man. She smiled, caressed his cheek, and lay back.

Then up the beach came the young woman's friends, and having put on shorts and T shirts, tying up the laces of enormous boots, they clambered up the cliff face, quickly reached a narrow path, and disappeared among the trees at the top.

Private again, and coming on strong now, he brought his head down to hers, and snogged her, a familiar movement this, part of their ritual. She only had to laugh now and he would stop, knowing she wasn't in the mood, but she was. So she allowed it, while at the same time pretending it was all him and nothing to do with her, the hard whore.

Then he pulled away, hard too: hard face, hard penis.

Sitting up, she stared defiantly back, putting her hand to her hair, lifting the tresses, looking knowingly, callously at him, tantalising him still, shaking it a bit, like the girl had shaken hers.

She could see that his need was prompting strong from below now. Driven on by her, forgetting the girl with the corkscrews, he wanted her desperately, wanted her for the passion of her defiance, for her goading, and for her bleached sexiness.

He reached down and undid the top of the tight denim shorts she was wearing, accentuating her curves and the pert bottom, and undid the zip before grasping her between the legs, over the rough texture of the cloth, and massaging her.

She looked sulky but let him do it, closing her eyes and surrendering to the feelings of pleasure her body was giving her.

Then he grabbed the tight T shirt, and pulled it up, she lifting her arms just enough for its removal, he having to force it a bit over her elbows, wrench it off her hands. Then she passively watched as he stroked the bra with the back of his hand, the necessary bra, something she had to wear, like the bleach. She had been reluctant to wear it this morning, although he knew she would in the end. To bait him she had offered excuses when he'd gone to her drawer, taken it out as she was dressing, and thrown it at her.

'Not today. It's too hot.'

'Wear it.'

'Not just for a boat trip. You're obsessed.'

And she had thrown it back at him. It fell short, on the floor. He had collected it and wordlessly thrown it back at her again, and it wrapped itself ludicrously round her face. Then she, slowly, deliberately, had unwrapped it, and with a pout, put it on. He had betrayed his feeling of male victory in that moment, smiling as at last her breasts stood out as they should, lifted into that special look he liked, real boobs, not just any old pair any more. And she had felt the whore, and enjoyed that, savouring her power to excite the male and proud too that she had got her man, despite all his macho crap.

Now he was looking at them there on the beach, encased, even in the heat, the large breasts. Massaging them and fondling them, feeling the crispness of the bra against the flesh. It excited her to see him do this and she pouted more and thrust them at him.

Then he got up, pulled out the parasol from the sand and threw it aside, and stood back away from her, ostentatiously showing her his prick, massaging it, bending it, demonstrating its hardness, knowing how she would respond.

And looking at it, feeling the swell of her desire, she cursed this thing of hers about pricks. She only had to see one and she was away. And knowing he knew that, knew her too well, knowing her fantasies about big pricks pushing at her, in libraries, at football matches, demanding her, forcing her, she moved towards it, knowing this one, knowing every vein every ridge and still wanting it. It had never lost its power, but knowing too his need to have her do this, so flouncing a bit, letting the opened front of her shorts flap, the boobs wobble, coming to it, taking it, knowing all the time what he wanted but refusing for now. Instead, she looked him in the eye, the two of them now anonymous in their sexual desire, he could be anyone, she could be anyone.

And then came a flash of the first time, there in the bar, she newly employed and at the end of her first night's work. The place had been almost empty at four a.m. with just a couple of friends of his left, and she had looked at him in that moment, wanted him, given the sullen come-on. And he really could have been anyone then. And he'd understood, and put down the glasses he was carrying and looked back, and so slowly, she could see it now, like it was slow motion, undone his belt and unzipped his trousers and taken it out so she could see how big and hard it was for her. And she'd done then, right there in public, what she was doing now, gone to it and gone on bended knees in front of it.

And still she made him wait. Kneeling in front of him on the hot sand, she stroked it with one hand, looked at it critically, as if she could choose to bite it off, him vulnerable now, feeling its strength and stiffness in its need for her, smooth, silky skin on it, so swollen with veins, then suddenly relenting and putting her mouth round it, feeling it both hard and soft in her mouth, feeling the ridges with her tongue, then pulling away, allowing it to slide out slowly through her lips, making the most of it, then bounce up in front of her face before lowering her head and putting her hand up to press it against her blondness, hearing him gasp then, sudden intake of breath, pleased with this touch, her knowledge of him, moving her head from side to side so it rolled across the cool, silky hair, then up again suddenly with her head and sucking on it hard, and he then grabbing at her in his lust, bunching her hair, the blonde, blonde hair in one hand so he had power now, took it from her, held her by a bunch of white stems, and shifting his weight fucked her mouth, she having to reach up to the hips to steady herself but not wanting to stop his penetration, letting it go right to the back, hard and needy in-out-in-out, before it was whipped away and she was back on the sand, on her elbows looking up at him like a picture from the movies - he would like that - pouting and ready.

Then him standing there, still for a moment, deciding what comes next, enjoying his machismo, she waiting and sort of guessing, knowing his favourites.

'Turn over.'

And this was the same as the first time, too. He'd stood there as now, looking at her with all the blackness of his desire on his face, as now, and issued the order.

'Turn over.'

And she, with a pout of resentment and a knowing look, now as then, pausing for a bit just to let him wonder if she really would do it and of course she would, he knew that, but it was all about timing, moving her head back to let the bleached hair dangle a bit, pushing up the breasts so they thrust a bit, calculated and cynical because she knew he liked it that way, to excite him, get him going.

Then ever so slowly she turned so he got her back end, the look of the back of the bleach, cut to just above the shoulders which were smooth and white, and pushed her rump up for him, exciting herself with this, getting more excited all the time.

Then she could feel one hand on her back, the other roughly pulling down the shorts to discover: no knickers. Deliberate that, just for this and she knew too what no knickers did for him, had them in her bag for after, pulling down the shorts, just far enough to expose her backside, round and womanly. Then she could feel him stroking it, like a piece of loved meat. She lowered herself down then, head resting on her arms on the sand, to brace herself.

And she remembered again the first time in the bar. She'd turned for him, but then it had been the dress she was wearing with no knickers, straight out of that film with Marilyn singing 'My Heart Belongs to Daddy'.

So all he'd had to do was pull the dress up and push in. He'd found her moist and ready and wonderfully tight. As now. What a hole. Best hole ever this one. Known that from the first time. Somehow gripped and massaged all at once, exciting the cock so it exploded with joy. But knowing too this was their tragedy, the bit that didn't work, the sorrow for both of them. Frigid. It had been hurled at her so many times. Why was this, this inability to go any further? Always excited, moist and ready, and then - nothing. Why was this tightness? Parents bloody parents, always tight at home around sex and she tight then around it, too many thoughts too much intellect, got to shut it out.

And he worked it, taking his time, in now, after pushing in to that warm place. She could sense him concentrating on himself, his own pleasure, trusting she would find hers in her own private way and remembering as she did that first time again. They were both facing a large mirror at one end of the bar and she'd watched him take her, excited by the extremity of her blondness, the totality of the image, she watching impassively with sulky mouth as he finished in so few strokes - bang, bang, bang - amazed and driven on by the tightness of her, so unexpected for one who looked so used and she amazed by her attractiveness, so new, the power it gave, feeling she could have any man now, just had to look and they'd come running, just like Marilyn.

And she loving that feeling of the penis, its ability to penetrate, thaw her if only a little bit. Tight in there, tight and warm. Working it, first in, now out, now round, no hurry, just easing it and working it.

Then suddenly spurred on, perhaps catching sight of the new whiteness of the hair as she raised her head slightly to get a better position, thrusting hard, leaning right over her to grasp the smooth tresses, thrusting quicker and harder until he reached the point of no return, relaxing then to allow the orgasm its own time to build, then aware of his moment of annihilation, because of his gasp and groan, which this image-making, this bleaching and bra-ing of her was all about, and then pulsating in his ejaculations until empty, not long, then pulling out, and slumping back on the beach.

She knowing all this, feeling it all, resigned because anyway it's all the same the next bit, closing her eyes so as to pretend to be in her own world, so no one's there, only her, the only way that was possible for her, concentrating on only one thing, allowing the sensations to build.

And then trying the favourite one, the football fantasy, standing there watching the game, and feeling it from the anonymous faceless man, the prick pushing, forcing its way in, her not moving, letting it, him doing and doing - in - in - in - and there it was, she came at last, sweating in the heat, on the hot sand. She thanked God it wasn't failure this time because she needed it, the shuddering and the oblivion.

He watched her idly as he searched for his cigarettes and lit one, noting the small cry from her as she peaked, and how she shuddered and tightened in little bursts, which slowly subsided. It was a good one today, he could see that.

He sat looking out over the green waters lapping at the edge of the little beach, cut so deeply in a narrow cleft of grey rocks - *smaragdi*, they called this colour, the colour of the clear waters, that special green that might also be blue but wasn't turquoise either - brilliant *smaragdi* - special.

And he remembered the first time, too, how he'd got it out for her, and how she'd come to it, and how, confident then, he'd told her to turn. It was in that moment he'd realised that this was the woman for him. After, left her and got on with clearing the tables and she was still there, crouched forward on the floor. And she'd got on with pleasuring herself, not caring who saw. He'd had an orgasm and now it was her turn: pushed herself and done it.

Why this was, he was wondering, too, but in a mild way, because the reality was that it was pointless to bother about such things. Her thinking about it only made it worse. Such things just were. So there would be a bit of excitement and then nothing more? So she never ever quite climaxed in the presence of a man? OK. It was the way of things. So she would have to go into her own world, pretend no one was there and do herself as if she was alone, then it would come, and only then? OK. He let her do it then, he let her do it now. Anyway, she insisted on it. Maybe if she didn't insist so much she would get one - but then, she was Northern European, you couldn't tell them these things, they insisted all the time.

Then he was aware at last that she had lain down beside him, and was lighting her own cigarette. He didn't have to make conversation. And she knew she could take off the bra now and she did. She could be naked now because it just didn't matter anymore. And she knew, too, that conversation was pointless. He'd taught her that. They were a couple. You knew everything, so what was there to say? All you had to do was be there, enjoying life, enjoying being together.

8. A One Night Stand

1

A 'beaut' was sitting at the bar above. He was aware of it as he descended the steep slope down to the little stream. He had heard her laugh: somehow light, youthful, modest and embarrassed all at once, but also calculated, erotic. A woman who knew her attractiveness and could use it.

But he didn't hesitate, or even look, just noted it for later.

He showed them what there was to see, this group of over-fifties, all so polite and obediently wearing their group badge. They were impressed, as always, by the sight of the Venetian lion at the stone tank, once, perhaps, with water coming out of its mouth, now neglected, ruins all around. He gave them his standard historical spiel about it all, then he ascended again, to the bar deep in the shade of a great plain tree. It was time to have a look at and enjoy the beauty.

What made a woman into a 'beaut'? He didn't really know - but either they were or they weren't. She had to be unique, he knew that, and striking: so striking that if she walked into a room heads would turn and look. This strikingness emerged from what she chose to wear, how she wore her hair, the nobility with which she carried herself. Warmth and zest for life radiated from her every gesture, every look, every word she spoke. And her mind was sharp and aware. But there had to be something else as well, a sense of her sexuality and allure for men. A 'beaut' knew about her charms, but didn't have to overtly parade them all the time. She was in touch with both her intellect and her deepest animal self and there was no conflict between the two.

Yes, there she was, and she was definitely a beaut.

She was with a group, two men and a woman, all young and chattering in French. All were in motorcycle leathers and were about to put on bright red identical helmets.

She had her back to him. She was slim, and had a spectacularly abundant mass of dark hair falling on her shoulders and tumbling in corkscrew curls down her back almost to its middle. Then suddenly she laughed again and it thrilled him.

The young man she appeared to be with was also beautiful but there was a subtle reservation in her manner which showed that this was some kind of temporary arrangement. She was enjoying him, allowing him to enjoy her too, but just for now. It pleased him. It meant she might be available to the right man.

She turned at that moment and caught his eye, looking briefly at him looking at her. Because of the depth of shade, with bright light behind, he could not tell her age or much about her looks. It didn't matter, she was still a beaut. Beauts were not beauts because of some standard of age or good looks but because of how they transformed themselves into beauty. Most were under forty but he'd known some incredible beauts in his time who by any regular standards would be considered ugly and old, but they'd used their looks in such an amazing way, carried themselves so wonderfully, that men fell at their feet - they were beauts.

It was a longish moment of eye contact. She didn't react, she wouldn't be a beaut if she did - she would expect to be looked at. Just that she looked and took in his gaze. In this his only motive was to affirm her beauty, let her know, feel a little prouder of what she was.

Then she turned and putting on a motorcycle helmet went to a big bike parked nearby and got on the back. The young man with her got on the driver's seat, and with a roar they were gone. The other couple followed almost immediately after. Avoiding the over-fifties, no doubt, in their youthful prejudice and not seeing the beauty and joy they too could bring to living. He could hear them larking about in the stream below, and a photograph being organised.

Later he would take them to the waterfall in its moist grotto and the cave in the cliff, high above the sea, with its mysterious paintings. He would tell them of seas swarming with pirates, people hiding and praying in this very cave while their loved ones were being slaughtered or carried off into slavery above them. How once, when Barbarossa attacked, they were hunted down even in their deepest sanctuaries and slaughtered, the women killing their children by throwing them over the precipice and then jumping after them rather than meet their fate. They would admire it all and be so grateful it wasn't them. Then next week another lot. He never got tired of it: sometimes, maybe, when there were complaints or the weather broke at the beginning or end of the season. It was fun. He enjoyed his job. Nor did he ever tire of the sights he showed them - they were perennially beautiful and always changing in little ways, with the season, with the people. Always some new detail he hadn't appreciated before or was appreciating again.

Later that day he saw the beaut again, one always did on a small island, and it came about in an unusual way.

Back at the hotel he'd sat down to watch the evening Greek lesson, which was outside in a shady courtyard, and of course the over-fifties loved to have him there and made a party of it. He raised his drink to them.

He'd sat himself down at the top of a flight of steps. It wasn't long before the owner passed on his way to his office, followed by a young woman. He'd not bothered to look properly because he'd assumed it was one of Yannis's hugely extended family. It was only when he heard the laugh again, coming from the direction of the office, that he'd realised and become alert. He couldn't see, because of a corner of the building, but he knew Yannis would be trying it on and it would amuse her. Then she'd returned, having delivered her passport, presumably, and some money. Yannis was always careful with bikers. She passed very close to him, but he'd been exchanging a joke in Greek with one of the over-fifties and so missed her. So she'd gone on, down the steps. He watched her, idly. Yes, it was the beaut from earlier in the day. Why had he not recognised her? Her hair was tied back, that's what it was. He noted how she held out slim, long, tanned arms to daintily balance herself as she went down the steps. He also noted how shapely were her hips encased in their tight blue jeans and how slim her waist was with its tight, wide, black belt . Above was a brilliantly cooured T shirt cut in sharply at the shoulders so as to expose the smooth, brown skin of her upper back.

This was always a feature of beauts, this choice of image, so precise and so simple at the same time, and it never failed to excite his desire, as it did now. It had always been like this. He could remember as a young child at school being fascinated by his first teacher, who wore kiss curls and flared, starched dresses. How mysterious and attractive it had seemed, this image that never seemed to vary and was always in perfect order. And he had noted, too, how the male teachers responded, found excuses to be in her classroom, courted her in a special way. How tearful he'd been when she'd left.

She'd stopped at the bottom of the steps and seemed to be hesitating, looking for her way. There was a burst of laughter from the group and the young woman turned quickly and looked back up the steps. She was pretty, the face was rounded, the cheeks full, and it had had an impish quality to it, and the eyes warm and brown.

There was a kind of searching expression, her forehead slightly wrinkled, until she saw he was looking at her. Then she smiled again. He raised his glass slightly, and the smile broadened. He saw her nod to him in response, and her eyes flick upwards to take in his balding head, with its cropped dark hairs and high forehead, before she walked daintily on again towards her room, sure of her direction now. There was an oddity about her, he realised - her eyebrows were left unplucked and met in the middle, and there had been the slightest hint of a moustache on her upper lip. But somehow it suited her.

He turned back to the class, and his eye was caught by Mary, one of the over-fifties who had taken a liking to him. She was fat and comfortable, and she knew how to enjoy life. He liked her, but evaded her advances. She winked her understanding of what had just passed. He blushed. Here he was, just turned forty and blushing!

But he wasn't going to chase the girl. He never chased women. It seemed undignified to him. No, he just let things happen. He was a philosopher, an enjoyer of life. True, he had done his share of chasing, especially in the navy. He'd had good time girls and prostitutes, at home and in foreign ports - dozens. But he'd moved on from all that once in his thirties, begun to appreciate a woman first as one would a good wine, reserving himself more, and later, very much later, some time during his period when he'd worked on the cruise ships, as people. That's when he'd created the concept of beauts: and how few there were on the cruise ships, though many tried. Why had he never selected a beaut for himself and settled down? That was a conundrum he'd never resolved. Something about responsibility. Needing to move on, not only from place to place but person to person. How could you be sure a beaut would stay a beaut? They might get terribly ugly the moment they put on that ring. Oh no.

It was a surprise to him, a couple of hours later, when he was in the bar of the hotel, sharing a drink and a chat with Yannis who was now acting as bartender, when the beaut appeared, on her own.

There was a brittle laugh behind him as she thanked someone for a compliment, and then she was next to him, asking Yannis for a coke. He noticed that she brushed lightly against him. She had changed, too. Now she was wearing a dress - white, like he was in white. He liked that. It was very slightly see-through, too, and he could just make out the outline of her body underneath, slim and delicate. Her hair was down again, and fell from her shoulders in thick, dark, waxy curls. There was the tiniest amount of tension and excitement about her now and it quickened his interest. He looked at her, not moving, and she turned to him and smiled again. He was aware of the tense brightness of the chestnut eyes, the nervous smile, the slightness of her build. He noticed how her hair was parted in the middle, and finished in a widow's peak low on her forehead. And the curiously heavy dark eyebrows, which stood out starkly. As he'd noted before, they were left natural and untrimmed, and met in the middle in an unruly display of short hairs. And he'd been right about the slight moustache on her upper lip, too. And yes, he liked this about her.

How old was she? Twenty? Probably. He waited to see if she would speak. Would she, or wouldn't she?

'You're the man with the group learning Greek.' She said it in French and he replied in the same language.

'That's right. And you're with the group on motorbikes.'

The coke arrived and she sipped it.

'Where are your friends?'

'They went off for something to eat and then they're going to the disco.'

She hadn't gone with them because she didn't feel well before, but she was better now. It had been a long journey to the island.

'And I needed a little time on my own. Things to do. You know, girl's things, to be beautiful.'

'You're very lovely.'

She smiled. Now she was silent, looking intensely at him. He realised they were studying each other. Then her smile broadened into unashamed delight as she seemed to realise almost at the same time as he did that there was desire between them and that it was mutual.

He got bold, took a risk. He reached out and ran his finger along the dark fur on the forearm she had shown. It was black and soft. She made no response except for a little giggle so he reached up and ran his finger lightly along the line of her widow's peak, then down the forehead and along the thick eyebrows, feeling the springiness of the bristles, especially at the point where they met. This he stroked several times. Again no response, just a further brightening of the eyes, an intensification of the smile, so he ran his finger down her nose and along the moustache on her upper lip, the hairs here so light and soft to the touch.

Now the act was repeated, but in reverse, first a stroking of his weathered arm with its tattoo, very traditional, an anchor, then the eyes flicked up to his pate and that was stroked, then his eyebrows, where she lingered on the nothingness in the middle.

'I pluck them'

She giggling at this admission, and moving on down to his absence of moustache.

'I shave.'

And then grabbing her finger for a moment in his teeth to show his readiness for her.

Then another giggle as she looked down modestly then up again into his eyes. She was excited, embarrassed and victorious all at once.

'Shall we go to my room? Would you like to?' It was simple and direct. He nodded.

'I'll get you another drink.'

He got the drinks and followed her. The members of his group who were present in the bar, and with whom he'd been having a social chat that evening, would assume they were going onto the lower terrace.

They reached her room and he followed her in.

It was plain, as they all were, white walls, twin pine beds and a few sticks of furniture. The bed was a mess, there were clothes everywhere, and the dressing table was piled with cosmetics, bottles of sun lotion, and junk.

He put the drinks down on the dressing table, pushing some junk aside to make space, then turned to her.

She stood squarely in front of him, about six feet away. First she kicked off her sandals then in a very no-nonsense way, stripped off the dress and stood a moment for inspection.

He knew she was flat at the front but was surprised by just how flat her breasts were. They were just the very slightest of swellings on her thin, bony torso with ribs showing, a strange contrast to the womanly roundness of the hips below.

She was clearly proud of how flat her chest was because

when she saw him looking, she ran her hands up her front to the nipples, tweaked them, and laughed.

Now more surprise. He knew and could see how hairy she was, but the growth of pubic hair between her legs was untamed and enormous - a triangle of black wires stretching almost from one hip to the other.

Now she was moving, trying to be natural in her nakedness, not quite succeeding. He was standing next to the dressing table, and she went up to it, close to him now. She took a sip from her drink, then turned away from him towards the dressing-table mirror, looking at herself curiously.

'Strange, aren't I? Not beautiful at all.'

The way she said it, he could tell she didn't believe this for a moment. She loved herself and knew she was very beautiful.

Moving behind her he pulled the thick mass of her hair aside and put his lips to the neck. There was a heady aroma about her of oriental spices. It exuded from her skin, it hung in her hair, and it excited him. The neck was long and slender and he worked over it with his lips and tongue, from the shoulders right up to the nape where her hair began. He could feel her beginning to tremble, and he was too. His passion taking over, he began licking higher up, working round to an ear, which he bit suddenly.

Now she was instructing him, urgently.

'You can spank me. I like that.'

He thrust three fingers, held hard and straight, into her mouth to shut her up, pushing them in and out like a penis as he buried his head in her hair, so scented and thick, eating it, worked his tongue over the sides and top of her head, she squealing and sucking harder every time the fingers thrust in, urging him on.

Finally he was twisting her head sharply round and licking the widow's peak and went on, holding her light body flat against him so that her backside pressed against his penis through the cloth of his shorts, licked his way along her eyebrows, glorying in their vigorous growth, especially the bit where they joined, and then went on down to kiss and lick the eyes, which she closed for him, then down the nose to the moustache, so soft and furry, and then had his fingers out of her mouth, was kissing her mouth hard with his mouth, thrusting his tongue deep inside while the free hand travelled down the front of her body, briefly flicking and massaging the nipples on the flat chest so they were erect and then on down over the flat belly into the black forest, and finding that yes there was a hole, and yes it was open and moist, ready for him as he thrust the fingers in and out a few times before seeking out, aware of his expertise, the clitoris, and working on it with his fingers until he felt her begin to shiver and stiffen, then pulling his mouth away and twisting her head back towards the mirror so she could see herself, glory in her strange hairiness as he brought her to a climax, simply holding her as she shivered and bucked in the throws of her orgasm.

Then he'd swept the dressing table clean of its rubbish, the objects clattering on the marble floor, pushing her forward looking at herself in the mirror with her rump presented for him, then leaving her there in anticipation, bent over the dressing table, face almost against the mirror while he undressed leisurely. Once naked, he stood behind her, erection jutting out awkwardly.

'You've been a naughty, sexy girl,' he said.

'Yes I have. I went to the bar and I picked up a strange man and I brought him to my room.'

She giggled briefly, then was serious again.

'Do it hard.'

He swung the flat of his hand hard against her buttocks several times leaving large red welts. Each time the hand met her soft flesh, she emitted a short gasp.

'More. Do it more. Harder.'

After twenty or so blows he was sweating, and his hand hurt. Her backside was scarlet and her breath was was coming in gasps.

Desperate for relief now he found his condom, and rolled it on. He could see she knew what was coming because she put her hands on the mirror to brace herself.

Grasping a bunch of the dark tangles somewhere near the crown, he flattened her mouth and nose against the mirror, and with the other hand guided his cock to the moist and ready entrance. Then he was in, and thrust hard, hearing the dressing table rattle and thump against the wall. He repeated the action several times then, feeling himself near to coming, he withdrew and pulled her towards him, then pushed her backwards, holding her so as to lower her onto the floor. Then wanting to be tough for her, dropped her the last bit of the way. Her head hit with a thud he hadn't intended but she didn't seem to notice.

He fell with his full weight on the fragile-seeming body but found it strong and sinuous. Strong arms were round him and he was being kissed, and her hands were massaging the baldness of his head as he entered her again, wet and urgent for him, and they bucked and thrust against each other, he again surprised by her - her pelvis moving with such power, and she quickly climaxing again, intensively with cries for mercy this time, and he came a little after.

When he'd caught his breath, feeling peaceful and fulfilled after the slaking of their lust, they got on the bed and sipped their drinks and chatted about their jobs, their lives, and everything, he listening to her, affirming her, and bringing her out till she was radiant and until they wanted each other again and this time it was different. They gloried without shame on the details of each other, licking freckles, kissing moles. Laughing, being affectionate, being tender. It was how he would want it if he ever did have a partner, but was it possible? Probably not. Only possible, for him anyway, if you had it in these brief encounters in which two human beings, after all the crap and urgency, could finally meet and just be. And tomorrow, or in an hour maybe, it would all be different, the crap would be back, but it was worth it, worth being alive, just for this, just for these moments. And such moments didn't, he realised, have to be preceded by sex all the time. Maybe if he just laid back even more, was just himself with people, drew them out, affirmed them, just as he had done earlier with her, these moments of pure closeness and intimacy could happen in all sorts of different ways, in shops, in bus stations, over a drink, anytime, if you were looking for them, the real joy of life, which was beyond trying and was about being.

Then it was time for him to leave and he went - no fuss.

2

She lay on the bed with the wreckage of the evening all around. It had been passionate, no doubt about that. And with an Englishman. Surprise, surprise. There was a sore lump on the back of her head where she must have hit it, although she had no recollection of that, her joints ached, and her bum was red and sore. She realised that when Michelle got home she might get another spanking. Beaten and ravished a second tme for being so naughty. She would enjoy that. Michelle knew how to do it because she had trained him well. But you could never tell with Michelle. He might return so drunk that he fell asleep without noticing. Or worse, just laugh and refuse to play.

She went back over the events of the day.

Along with Michelle and the others she'd been sitting under the big tree with coffee, when they'd heard the party of laughing older people arrive. They disgusted her friends because of their ugliness and age. Also, they were English and had no sense of style. People with no style angered them.

They'd spent a few moments exchanging sneers about the new arrivals who hadn't come immediately to the bar, preferring to go down to the stream. But her friends decided to leave, knowing that the group would be along shortly, and their idyll would be destroyed. She herself was intrigued and would have stayed.

She was about to get on the back of Michelle's big bike, when she had looked round for some reason and caught what appeared to be the leader of the group, who'd come early up to the bar, looking at her. She had vaguely noticed the tall figure with the group because his baldness reminded her of her father. She was in that stage of grief when you seem to see the lost person everywhere, are about to respond, and then realise with disappointment that it is not possible. It is someone else. When she had looked at him, he hadn't flinched or gone embarrassed as men often did, but simply carried on looking. And she had looked back and realised that she too was attracted. Her father had been bald and their relationship, so tough and playful, had been more a love affair really. She had led him on, enticing him endlessly with her naughtiness. And the spankings he gave! When had she realised that she actually wanted them, that they were part of the pleasure of her intimacy with him? And later, when he had realised what was going on, and had had to hold himself back, how she had longed for him to do it, seen his longing, but understood, too, that he couldn't. So she had put her arms around him, kissed the bald head and decided she must find other partners to play with. But this had only deepened their bond. Yes it had been lovely all that, and her mother so jealous really, though she tried to hide it. It was now exactly one month since he was killed in a road accident.

So, there in the village square she had registered the man, and had then turned away to put on her helmet, but nevertheless a little shiver of sexual arousal had gone through her. The man was old, but lean and athletic. He was tanned. She had wanted him.

They had arrived at the hotel looking for a room for the night. She had volunteered to see what was available. She'd found the proprietor working in his garden and had been shown a studio with two bedrooms, but without a balcony and they would have to share facilities. Since the price was not high between the four of them, she had called the others in and they had taken it. They had had a bit of time to settle in, and it was perhaps an hour later when the proprietor reappeared and asked her to follow him with her passport to the office to carry out necessary formalities.

He had selected her for this honour because he was attracted to her, she could see that. Yes, the man - Yannis, wasn't it? - wanted her, but she wasn't at all attracted. This was a fat slob. The other one this morning, though, had been different. Lean, oldish perhaps, but also insolent in his knowledge of his beauty in not looking away. That was her father: knowing and skilful with women. He had known she would want him, the bastard. Following the slob and trying to ignore his chatter in English, a language which she hated and had never really made more than a passing effort at, she had been surprised to find their route took them past the old people sitting in a group. A little apart from them was the leader who'd looked at her in the morning, the bald head displayed for all to see, and it gave her a little thrill immediately.

He didn't try to hide it, like some, so he must like it. She hated it when they tried to cover it up with long unsuccessful tendrils from the back or side, and she was turned off. The slob did that. No, they had to like it, to glory in it, as her father had. Then and only then was it attractive.

There was a moment when he glanced up and greeted the proprietor, but he hadn't looked in her direction. That had been a disappointment.

As she returned from the office she went right past him, very close, but again he hadn't looked towards her because he was engaged by the group. But she had the opportunity to take in his lean, bronzed features, the brown scalp with its short dark hairs at the sides, so like her father's. He was wearing all white for the evening with his shirt open at the front. She could just see dark curls of hair on the chest. She had wanted him even more now and was desperate to do something to attract his attention. She gave her pelvis an added swing as she descended the steps. Maybe she could pretend to have forgotten something, or needed to know the way. She'd hesitated. But then she'd heard laughter from the group behind her and turned.

Now he was looking at her, and she'd caught his eye. She'd let him see that he was acceptable by smiling, and he raised his glass. Satisfied for the moment with her success, she'd walked on, but also at the same time deciding that now she had to find a way of breaking away from the others.

In fact, when she'd got back to the room they were impatient to be off to another part of the island for the evening. It turned out there was some life there, a disco. It was dead here. She'd feigned a headache and they'd left her almost immediately. Michelle, she'd realised, would be eager to find talent that suited his own tastes in this new playground. But that was Michelle. He would do it anyway, whether she was there or not. He never let her presence inhibit his style if there was something or someone he wanted.

Then she'd been confronted with a new problem. How was she to present herself this evening? She had one dress with her which could be very becoming. She had bought it in of all places Marks and Spencers in Paris, just wandering round out of curiosity and seen it among all the outrageous English styleless crap. So white, so short on her tall frame, it showed off her elegance and her youth. And it was just see-through, so people were able to just see her nipples, and looking down, the faintest dark mass at her crotch. It was both girlish and sexy. It was how Daddy liked her, in a short dress, though these days she rarely wore one. Yes, she would wear it tonight. Would she go so far as make-up? She had it with her, just in case. Why not? Might as well go all the way. Some of the very special scent she had with her that Daddy liked, and long ear-rings, and would her hair be up or down? Daddy liked down, so down it was.

Then she was ready and she had to find him. No time like the present, so she'd left the room. Her plan had been simple: they were in a small place, so all she had to do was wander from bar to bar. If he was around she would find him. If not, she wouldn't. She'd gone first to the hotel bar, the obvious place. And it was easy because there he was on a high stool talking with the slob, who was serving. She'd headed in that direction. Some fool of an English woman tried to engage her with compliments on the way across the room, but she'd dismissed it quickly and moved on, coming right up beside him, allowing her dress to brush against him and sat down on the next stool. He would get the full blast of her warmth and the scent of her newly showered body, and look at her.

A little over-doing it in her nervous energy, she'd ordered a Coke. The slob tried smiling at her, but she took no notice.

Waiting for her drink, she'd been able to sense he was indeed looking at her. She'd let him look and take it all in.

But now doubts had assailed her. He was English and English people had funny ways when it came to sex. They were embarrassed by it and if it was offered to them on a plate like this were very likely to run away.

And then there was a sudden new doubt. Did she really want *him*? English men were either gentlemanly idiots or lager-swilling brutes. She wanted neither. And how attractive was he really? This was her first opportunity to be close to him. This close, when she could actually get the texture of him she might not want him. He might not even be available - she hadn't thought of that. And the converse was true. This was was his first chance to really get a close look at her. She was confident of the profile he was getting now, but when she turned to him he would get the full blast of the eyebrows and the moustache. How would he take that? Although she saw them as attractive, English men were supposed to like their women plucked and shaved. And he would be able to estimate just how non-existent were her tits. Again, English men were supposed to like them big.

He said nothing, so she turned to him. He had marvelously blue eyes, both gentle and intense, and also with a touch of humour and delight in them as they studied her. She'd not noticed before but he had a ring in one ear. It was a confident, unashamed face she was looking into, an experienced face. It had seen and enjoyed many women, many tastes. There was a touch of sadness there, too.

He showed no signs of hurry, so, a little excited and nervous, she came out with a few phrases in French about knowing who he was, forgetting that he probably wouldn't understand her and she would have to struggle with English.

But no, he had smoothly replied in French, and said it in such a way as to leave no room for misunderstanding. He had seen her, too, and the way he accented it encouraged her to think that he had admired and wanted her. He'd asked about her friends and she'd said they'd gone off and she'd stayed because she'd not felt well.

She'd immediately started talking again and changed the explanation, becoming the girl in need of personal space. And she'd done it well, she thought, but wasn't sure he'd been convinced. But it didn't matter, he didn't press her on it, as a younger, stupider man might, and blow the whole thing, on an issue like that. No, he'd made it nice for her, made it, somehow, a collusion.

And suddenly after the nervousness and the doubts she was enjoying it, knew they were at least talking now and it was good.

And then they had just stared at each other for a bit, enjoying what they saw, no point in speaking because they were in the power of the erotic and words would break the spell. Then he had reached out and touched her arm and she, in a dream-like state, had simply watched the finger caress the hairs there. Then the finger had got bolder and stroked her eyebrows and she had let it, and it had paid special attention to the little flower box of hairs in the centre, driving her crazy with the sensations it generated but still she had not moved, just let it run down her nose, and stroke her moustache.

Then it had been her turn to enjoy him with her finger. And she had traced the tattooed anchor on his arm, aware of his history without having to ask boring questions about it, after all, who cared, it wasn't the experiences that made a man it was the learning from them, the sum total that either did or didn't add up to something, more than the parts.

Then she was up stroking the longed-for pate and found it smooth as silk, the short hairs at the sides soft and pliable like down in their fineness, she using her whole hand, whereas he had only dared use a finger right at the front.

Then down to his brows, he admitting that his too met in the middle to her delight, and on down to his cleanly shaven cheeks towards his mouth.

Then the finger was held sharply and firmly between two sets of white teeth (were they false? she hoped desperately they weren't) and sucked in a very erotic way indeed, a promise for what was to come.

Now she was silent with expectation, suddenly a little modest and embarrassed, which was all to the good, because men wanted you like that. And it was all Daddy and Daughter play, and with real Daddy it had never gone any further, but with this one it could and she wanted it to. And she realised that during all this she had been getting moist and swollen down below and she needed to get things over because she had deliberately left off her knickers and she was afraid lest her moisture would stain the dress for everyone to see. Suddenly there was a rush to her head, and she knew she was blushing and afraid, and that it would come out awkwardly, but she had done it anyway.

She had suggested that they go to her room and he had accepted, and feeling elated and victorious she started to move immediately. She could sense no sign of moisture on the dress but she had to move fast, and waiting for him to buy two more drinks was torture, but she waited nevertheless and went out ahead of him - if there was a stain up the back, only he would see it from behind and it would drive him on.

Once in her room she realised what a mess it was, but it didn't matter. She'd wanted to get on with it so had stripped quickly, showing now the non-existent breasts, and trying to show him, through her own enjoyment of them with her hands, that they were beautiful too, just like enormous ones, if only you knew how to appreciate them.

Wanting him to get going, she had sought something to do and gone over to the dressing table, near him. She could feel his heat, and had taken a gulp from her drink. Then she was distracted by her image in the mirror and realised suddenly, as if he was the mirror, how strange she must seem to him. And a sudden doubt again, did he still desire her now he could see everything, blurting the words out in so many words, as she did in awkward moments, that she wasn't really beautiful.

But he hadn't rejected her, he'd just started to kiss and lick her neck, a surprise because it wasn't a part of her she'd ever thought about. And she realised also that he'd started and the game was over. But there were things she needed to say if she was to get full enjoyment so she started to blurt again, the tongue had now reached an ear and was exciting her further and further so it was difficult, she liked a sound fatherly spanking, so she said so, but very quickly fingers had been stuffed into her mouth and she was sucking on them, and she could already feel waves of pleasure flowing. Then he seemed to be finished slobbering her ear and slobbered her eyebrows and her eyes, no one had done this before but she enjoyed it. Then he was slobbering into her mouth uncontrollably and she was enjoying that too - God the English were so crude - and she felt her breasts caressed and then fingers in her down there and then unbearably having her clit done over until she was insane with pleasure, this wasn't crude at all, just what she needed, and suddenly she was held, looking in the mirror and glorying in her self as she orgasmed to it in wave after wave. And then it was a quiet time, God knows what he's doing, undressing probably, and then he'd said 'naughty girl' and she'd replied, begging for it hard to encourage him, thank God she'd found a man prepared to do it, you could never tell with Englishmen although beating was supposed to be English sex - why did she have all these quirks? Then there was a sharp slap across the buttocks, sort of punishment but play too, and again and again and she was stinging with it, and demanded more and harder, and got more, till it was all glorious sting. Then it had stopped, and, looking round, she could see him casually rolling on a condom and it was a big one, my God, an Englishman with a big one! and she knew what she was in for, and she was pleased and braced herself for it, because after what she'd said there would be no preparation. She put up her rump as high as she could to receive and in it came, deep and splitting with her head forced hard against the mirror she couldn't see and enjoy herself as she would have liked to. Then this was over and it was out and then she found her back hard against the cold marble of the floor, so unyielding, and she loved this too, and he was on her and in her again, so simple now, no frills just banging her as hard as he could and she was grabbing at and loving his baldness as she banged back, saying Daddy, Daddy to herself, feeling suddenly a new orgasm coming like lightning and sweeping over her in an agony of screaming pleasure and he was left behind to take what pleasure he could in his own brief male orgasm. And then it was over, he was off her.

Then a real surprise. Like walking again with Daddy in the park. They'd talked. Is this something they did in England? Michelle never did. She'd liked it, she'd glowed. Just about this and that. Her hopes and fears. And yes it was strange her liking to be punished, perhaps her father shouldn't have been so erotic with her when he did it, although he hadn't gone all the way, but he might just as well - in some ways him stopping himself had only made it worse - and especially him dying like that.

And underneath, the talking was all about the joy of life, its beauty within its banality and you only had to look at it right to fully appreciate it. And somewhere along the line he'd called her a beaut and she'd known that anyway, but it was nice to know it again. And afterwards they'd made such gentle, beautiful love. How it was really with Daddy.

She was happy.

And thank God he was able to leave her at the right moment. Horrible when they doted on her and wanted to stay.

And then much later, with the light of a new day just breaking through and Michelle and the others not returned yet, her sexuality rising again it suddenly seemed not so bad after all to see him again. She'd already noted how they'd look good together if you didn't mind the age bit. Maybe she could persuade the others to stay one more night or she could get his address and visit him in England (God, what a place!), if he would let her stay, of course, for a while. He'd have to learn to be harder on her, though, the spanking in retrospect hadn't gone on nearly long enough, but he was good with the clit and the straight stuff, no doubt about that. And was he, back in his own room across the town, his own sexuality rising again, thinking similar thoughts?

9. The Insect

This is the story of how Jurg visited Aphrodite's island. He hadn't meant to, but he and his travelling companion Heine had got drunk the night before, overslept, and missed their proper connection. A nearby ferry had been loading, seemed to need business, so they'd boarded, knowing this would have to be their last stop before turning their bikes northward to take up their medical studies in Germany again.

When they arrived, they scoured the place for rooms and found some cheap ones up in the old town. Jurg hunted for creepy-crawlies in all the darkest corners. He had a pathological fear of insects, and to his relief, apart from a line of ants that wound its way down a wall to feed on an old sandwich that had somehow got itself lodged behind a bedside table, they seemed very clean. Using a tissue to hold it, he threw the sandwich in the bin and wiped away the ants with a wet kitchen sponge. They then unpacked their swimming gear, and went straight down to the beach.

Stripped, and sunning themselves, they were assessing the talent when a huge hornet, all brown and yellow stripes, came buzzing slowly along to inspect them. Jurg waved it away, but it persisted, and he had to hit out at it with increasing fury and fear several times before it decided to back off and move on to more attractive pickings elsewhere. He was left breathless and nervous. He inspected the sand for bugs and the air for more insects. It was only when none appeared that he could begin to relax again.

Meanwhile Heine, who had been completely indifferent to the incident, had picked out a number of beauties already, and had become interested in one of two young women who stood in front of them in the sea.

'Look at the arse on her. And those legs! God, is she tall!'

Jurg had predicted which one he would want five minutes before. Heine always went for Amazons. That was his thing. If they were going to tower over him and bully him then he was interested.

'I bet when she turns round she's over forty and flat chested,' said Jurg. He felt he had to play along.

'If she is I'll suck your cock.'

There was no doubt she was a magnificent creature, tall and muscular, classically proportioned, tanned to a deep chocolate brown, with an abundance of jet black hair that streamed down her back and didn't finish until it was a foot below her rump. But then, Heine was also a magnificent creature, thought Jurg, with his open, regular face and muscular body, so carefully cultivated over the year, every day in the gym, his light brown hair bleached in natural-looking streaks, worn in corkscrews to his shoulders. He was just a bit short, that was all. It was a fact he could never come to terms with. That was why he liked tall people like the Amazon and Jurg himself.

Women always seemed to come in pairs: the pretty one and the ugly one. Jurg's role in the friendship was to befriend the ugly one. Not that he was particularly ugly himself. Dark, and enormously strong, if a bit flabby (he liked beer and didn't work out like Heine), he tended to scare women away. The benefit for him in this arrangement, therefore, was that at least he got Heine's rejects.

There was a fiction between them that they were equal, and could go for any woman they wished, even if that brought them into competition, but with Heine's looks it never worked out that way. And anyway, he would always intervene as he did now.

'I need you to give me room on this one. She's special. OK?'

They were always special.

'Sure. No problem.'

Suddenly Heine creased up with laughter.

'I don't think much of yours.'

Their attention shifted to the Amazon's companion.

'You know what she reminds me of? An insect.'

And it was true. Next to the Amazon, looking tiny and rather ridiculous by comparison, was another figure. The 'ugly one', who they could also only see from the rear, wasn't only rather small and slim, she was also a very strange shape. She had long, thin arms and legs and an extraordinarily short torso, which suddenly contracted into a wasp-thin waist, then just as suddenly opened out again to rather wide hips. She had a very small head, accentuated by the fact that her dark hair was slicked straight back into a shiny helmet which finished abruptly in a straight line at the nape, with a thin, tanned neck extending below it. To complete the effect, she was wearing swimming trunks with bright yellow and black stripes. So there she was: an insect complete in all its parts - head, thorax, abdomen and limbs, of which, fortunately, there appeared to be only four instead of the regulation six.

And then there were her movements: quick, wide gestures of the hands and of the legs which would suddenly stop in mid-flight. The effect was exactly that of an insect.

'See you.'

Heine had got up and now walked close past the young women and into the sea, pausing for a moment to allow them to inspect his beautifully proportioned body before plunging into the sea and moving fast away from the shore with his best crawl. This was the opening move, intended to let them know he was here. If they were still there when he returned, he might have a chance to show himself again, and maybe start something. Jurg had seen it all before.

Just then there was a roar of engines and another beauty arrived. This one was male, dark, very Greek, and in a speed boat. This he deftly manoeuvred between swimmers, and stopped right in front of the Amazon.

A few words were spoken and the Amazon got in. Jurg knew that Heine would not be put off at all by such an event. He quite liked competition, because he always won.

A rather brief offer was made to the insect, but she clearly refused (she knew her place) and the speedboat roared off towards the gigantic rock that stood, like a large egg, just outside the entrance to the bay. Jurg guessed that the Amazon was going to be shown the sea caves that existed on the rock and which were apparently a beautiful sight. He had read the guide carefully in advance and had himself planned an excursion there in a hired boat, possibly with girls and a picnic, should the opportunity arise.

His attention now turned idly back to the insect, who, after watching the boat for a few moments, rather elegantly lifted the long legs and turned to face the beach.

Jurg was frozen like a statue for a moment, eyes staring, mouth half open. He had seen her breasts. They were gigantic and displayed for everyone to see. For some reason it had not occurred to him that she was topless. Her friend had been, it was true, and he had seen her rather uninterestingly normal ones. He had somehow assumed that since Insect was the ugly one hers would be smaller. But they weren't. They were enormous, and so well formed, hanging down of course, because of their weight, but thrusting upwards and out, too, with the nipples almost vertical on the end, like the stalks on two huge melons, fat with nourishment and bursting with taste. They were so huge they looked as if God had, in a moment of distraction, stuck them on by mistake: they were really meant for the

Amazon, who'd only got the regulars when she should have got the XL's. And the effect was heightened by Insect's slight frame.

Breasts were Jurg's fetish, just as Amazons were Heine's. And just as for Heine the taller the better, for Jurg the bigger the better. How can I describe to you the effect on a breast-man of seeing a particularly enormous pair of breasts, or for that matter a leg man of seeing a particularly long pair of legs, a shoes-man of seeing particularly long heels, a long-hair-man a particularly long head of hair? Obviously if you do have a fetish you will know instantly, the intensity of pleasure, the weakening of the limbs, the annihilation of all reason. If you don't, let's try some psychology. When Jurg saw those breasts, the baby within him saw Mum. Imagine it. The young woman turns round and suddenly there's Mum! Wow! The object I most desire and love in the whole world! The fount of all wisdom and succour! Baby instantly reaches for it. It must have it. Now. Babies can't understand delay. Give it me!

And of course, don't forget that babies are erotic creatures. Freud was adamant on that point. Babies are having a love affair with Mum or, as in this case, her replacement. They experience her with avid use of all the senses and they get turned on.

Jurg from time to time would indulge his baby in the privacy of his room by buying big breast magazines and masturbating over them, loving the moment when his spunk spurted out all over the magazine, and, in fantasy, all over the breasts. Very baby-like behaviour, messy, but delightful if you really get into it and let go of the hang-up (usually inculcated by Mum, of course) that you shouldn't be a baby but Grown-Up.

But here he was on a beach. It was a social situation. He

couldn't just rush up to her as the inner baby was demanding. He had to control himself and just sit there, ogling her.

Ignoring Jurg, the young woman, in her rather jerky, insect-like manner, now walked up the beach, passing very close to Jurg, and even spraying him with a little salt water as she went by. He stared at her all the way, twisting his head right round, unable to take his eyes off her. She appeared not to notice. Simply went back to her sunbed, where she slumped down and opened a book, out of Jurg's line of sight for the moment.

Jurg was in the grip of a powerful lust that he rarely felt. An erection was growing and he knew he would have to do something about it.

He plunged into the sea and swam out strongly. It did for the erection, but he couldn't get the image of her out of his mind.

'I must have her. I must.'

Never mind about Heine and the Amazon. He knew what he wanted and it was her. Had one of the local Greeks picked her up and already taken her? Unlike Heine he didn't fancy his chances against a Greek because they were so beautiful and he just wasn't, but if, if she wasn't taken yet...

He knew what he had to do and he did it.

He went straight back to the shore, found Heine with eyes closed sunbathing, mumbled something, and went straight back to the room. There he wanted to take the edge off his lust by tossing himself off. If he didn't do this he was afraid he would have an embarrassing erection most of the rest of the day, and if an opportunity came to talk to her he would fluff it: he needed to be casual and calm.

But he couldn't do it. He tried to fantasise what it would feel like with her and that had caused a problem. The breasts he had no trouble with, they would be amazing. He could admire them, bury his head in them, lick them, bite the nipples, generally play outrageously with them. But the image of an insect kept intruding. What would the spindly arms and legs be like around him, the smooth, ball-like head to stroke? Would she encase him in a vice-like grip from which there was no escape, insert her mandibles into him and suck out his vital juices? Ridiculous, but it put him off. Basically she just wasn't attractive enough. He needed more in a woman than simply a pair of breasts. So he lay back and rested. Some time later he woke from semi-sleep with a start. There was a large centipede climbing the wall behind him. Slowly, he picked up a book from the bedside table and turned to look at it. It was horrible: a sort of red colour, long and thin, with many legs. He knew it was aware of being observed because it stopped moving and made a cracking sound as of electricity. He slammed the book down on it and pressed hard. When the book was removed the animal slithered lifeless to the floor and a dark stain appeared on the wall. He didn't dare pick the animal up. Looking at his watch, he realised that two hours had gone by. It was lunchtime. He got up and returned through the heat to the beach. As he suspected, Heine had gone. He reckoned that he was most likely having a beer. He picked up his stuff and went to look.

On the promenade behind the beach, there were a series of bars and restaurants. He saw Heine in what looked like the flashiest, supping beer and - yes - with him were the Amazon and the young Greek. At the table also was Insect.

He approached and sat down in one of the canvas chairs, feeling tense. Fortunately Insect's breasts were now covered, so he wouldn't be distracted by them. She was wearing a kind of loose sarong so fashioned that you wouldn't know what was under it. Not unless you'd already seen them on the beach. He decided to keep his distance from her. It was shady and cool in the bar, and Jurg relaxed a bit. Heine of course did not introduce him, but was absorbed in talking to the Amazon in German. The other two looked slightly left out, and were just sitting there silently. He ordered a beer for himself and made no effort to engage them in conversation. The more he kept his contact with the girl to the minimum the easier it would be. He occupied himself by watching yet another real insect, this time small, flat, bright green, and leaf-shaped, crawl across the table and drink at a puddle of beer. It then staggered in circles as if drunk. He lacked sufficient energy to attempt to kill it. At last his drink came and he lifted the bottle to his lips. As he did so he caught Insect's eye for a moment, and she smiled. He had to admit that it was a nice smile and he became aware of two big, humorous brown eyes in the same moment. The cool liquid slipped comfortingly down his throat. He didn't smile back.

'Are you with Heine?'

'Yes.'

'You're Jurg.'

'Yes.'

'I'm Dorothea.'

'Hi.'

'You arrived this morning.'

'Yes.'

'It's nice here. You'll like it.'

He had to admit it was a nice voice, too, sort of soft and gentle, and again there had been a touch of humour around, a kind of knowledge communicated, about what was going on with Heine and the Amazon, almost a camaraderie. He that maybe she wasn't so bad after all.

Also he had been so obsessed with her breasts that he had not been able to look at her face. But now he did so he realised that she was actually quite pretty.

She had big brown eyes framed by long lashes, which stood out sharply against the little pointed face with its delicate mouth and pixie nose. There were delicate, expressively arched eyebrows. The glossy, straight-back hairstyle now seemed so right for her. Unfortunately, the thin, brown, angular limbs and frame had lost none of their insect-like quality with closer viewing. She would move to drink her beer in little bursts, followed by long stillnesses. And she spoke nervously, in much the same way, in little bursts, with an irritating habit of laughing a short, nervous laugh at at the end of a sentence. It was like a cricket chirping. He hated crickets. He found out that, like Jurg and Heine, they were students from Germany who had travelled down to Greece for the summer.

That evening, Jurg panicked when, having a shower before going out with the girls to the disco, he looked between his feet and saw a baby scorpion, tail up, threatening to sting him. It wasn't clear which of them was the most afraid. Clutching his towel to his nether parts, he dashed, squealing with fear, to fetch Heine, who coolly killed the animal by hitting it with the heel of a shoe.

It took several beers before images of what might have been - hospital and even death - began to fade and he could pay proper attention to his companions. She was so bright and warm compared to the ponderous off-handedness of the other two, that he found himself warming to her even more. They had been irritated when he insisted on smarming evil-smelling bug repellent all over his exposed areas, but she just laughed and said she didn't mind a bite or two. Then there was a moment when he and Heine and the Amazon were sitting at their table and Dorothea was dancing on her own on a floor that had emptied, with Heine making more comments in his ear about her appearance, when he began to look at her in a new light altogether. Yes, she was an insect, no doubt about it, but such a delightful insect. When she danced, the long thin arms would jerk about, and so would the legs, the head would twist on its stalk, but it was all so perfect, such a display of insectness that he was won over by it. He couldn't take his eyes off her. Slowly, Jurg found himself filling with a sense tenderness for this delicate creature. She was all round such a nice person. She listened with focus and respect, and when she made a little joke, it wasn't at anyone's expense at all, more about life itself, and it made you feel better afterwards. And it was as if, as she questioned him, she was trying to bring him out, get him to be more of himself, less withdrawn and dependent on Heine. He made some positive comment and Heine was scathing immediately.

'You're not falling for her are you? That?'

'No, no, of course not,' he said hurriedly.

But he knew that he was. And it was very odd. He realised that he adored her insectness. He loved the long spindly limbs, the wasp-thin waist, the little ball of a head. They were gorgeous for what they were. And as for the mind inside, well, that was gorgeous, too. The thought of it made him glow.

And so he was watching her now, and she came to realise this, because she shot glances as she danced, and at first he looked away, only to start looking again immediately. But she caught him out so many times, and anyway, she seemed to be stealing glances at him as much as he was at her. In the end he stopped bothering to look away, just carried on staring at her, giving a smile when she looked, so she smiled too, and became even more insect-like, and sort of did her bit for him on the dance floor. And he liked this so much that he smiled even more and looked even harder till in the end it was just him and her, no one existed in the whole world except the two of them, even though in reality the floor was filling up again. The other two were sitting glumly beside him because it wasn't working for them, and they could see what was happening. And when the music stopped she came to sit down, not across from him, which she could have done, but right next to him, and suddenly they had an unspoken alliance and the other two could do nothing about it. They were the ugly ones now, who had to get along together somehow, for them. So they chatted, darting looks and appreciations, and they danced together and they danced apart, but whatever it was it was always with awareness of and for the other. It was a flirtation, the time before anything happens, and it's good to extend that time because it's so delightful, and it's over too soon anyway. It's that moment of certainty of being desired, but anxiety too because although you are certain, nothing's been said yet, so you're not really certain at all, and the feelings inside are so good about it and about life.

So as the dawn was coming up the men took the girls home on the backs of their big bikes. He made an arrangement with her to go swimming later in the day, and that was inevitable, though still a risk to do, as it always is, so he tried not to make too big a deal of it.

'How about a swim later? Go somewhere. You and me.'

'OK'

'See you then.'

'OK'

He spent a great deal of money on hiring a motorboat and took her out to the big rock outside the harbour. Here they drifted into the sea-cave, and sat and admired the blue light coming from under the surface. And it was a nice and peaceful time together, sort of friendly, and yes, that other was present, too, in this place, the very place, where Aphrodite was born, and her magic was all around. But he had made no effort to touch Dorothea. He had wanted to keep his distance until the moment came. The right moment.

Then they found a deserted little beach, hemmed in from behind by high cliffs and private from the sea because of a rock that guarded the entrance and turned the water into a smooth, emerald pool. And having swum, and played in it, and having dried off in the sun, they both modest in trunks, and she with her bikini top on, because they were alone together and were a bit shy yet and didn't want to give the wrong impression, he became aware of her beauty again, lying quietly on her back next to him, while he was on his front. With this awareness, he could feel his penis hardening, and therefore dared not turn over because it would show. He turned his head towards her and found her looking at him with her big eyes.

Now he found himself reaching out, very slowly, so as not to scare her. He raised one hand and gently stroked back a hair that had drifted forward over her face. Without taking her eyes off him, she made one of her endearing little nervous laughs, and he realised the moment had come.

He turned towards her, careless now of her seeing his erection - let her see, and know she was desired - but she never took her eyes off his. There was a light in them and a faint smile, and an expression of wonder and trust. He leaned over her, serious, and traced the line of her arched brows, then down her nose and round her mouth.

Suddenly there was another little laugh and he found his finger trapped between two sets of strong, sharp teeth. It hurt. The insect could bite.

'Ow!'

She looked at him as if to say she could bite the finger off in a moment if she chose. But slowly the expression changed. It became saucy, and, releasing the grip of her teeth, she took the finger deep into her mouth and sucked on it, then slowly withdrew from it, flicking out a long tongue and giving it a quick lick before pulling away. Still, her eyes never left his.

Then he was kissing her, mouth to mouth, deeply, releasing now all his longing, showing no mercy, holding the thin body tightly in his arms, seeking out, in his own time, all of it. First he ran his hand again over the glossy hair, and found it cool and strong and he loved the bit where it ended suddenly and he was stroking the so long neck, and down the taut back, finding how smooth her skin was, feeling and tracing the slimness of her waist and then down to the buttocks and how round and womanly they were compared to the rest of her, she squealing when he found them and stroked them. And feeling her bend her arms about him to gently stroke him, and finding them so caressful and delicate that it went beyond all belief and drove him crazy with desire.

Then, tentatively, in awe and wonder, he was releasing her bikini top, fumbling with his big fingers, and she, with a smile, pulled away and did the job for him, and her breasts flopped out, huge and heavy, and he bending forward to them, gently at first, hardly able to believe his luck, then more confidently and passionately, eating them, sucking them, with his mouth, squeezing them, manipulating them with his hands, glorying in them, until he could hear her breath coming in short gasps, and he left them to explore with kisses the flat stomach, then awkwardly pulling her trunks down, putting his head into the neatly clipped pubic hair and nuzzling its coarse darkness, before descending into the crevice between her legs searching for the clitoris, and at last finding the little knob and lying still now all except for tiny movements with his tongue. It was a gift of pure pleasure he wanted to give her. Then she was twisting herself, and crawling down him, so delicately, so lightly and insect-like, that he hardly noticed.

So it was a surprise to him when he suddenly he found his penis released from its prison, firmly gripped at the base and thrust deeply into the small mouth, so deep he could feel it pushing against the back of her throat, and a strong suction applied that thrilled and electrified him. Yes, she was going to suck his vital juices, but he wanted it so much, to be, if necessary, annihilated by this insect.

And thus they lay, for what seemed to them like hours, coupled as insects couple, but in actual fact it was only a few minutes.

Then they were apart for a moment, before, without hesitation now, he drew off his trunks completely, pulled away hers, put all his enormous weight onto the frail body and thrust the eagerness of his erection deeply into her, finding her ready and moist, her vibrating quickly under him almost immediately in violent orgasm with gasps and cries. Then he, to take his final pleasure in his own way, pulled out of her, and kneeling astride her, took the heavy voluptuousness of her breasts in his hands, pushed them together and thrust his penis between them, until the moment of no return came and he released them, pulled back a little from her, and seeing that her head was back, raised it for her to see, and allowed the pulses of spunk to spurt out over them in a moment of pure drama and joy.

And as the spurts subsided he spread his juice over them, tenderly, making them glisten in the sun. Then finally putting his sticky hand to her mouth, wiping it over, and she, laughing now, licking it off, and then he kissing her, the flavour of his own semen strong and salty.

And it happened very quickly. In just two days there he was looking into the big brown eyes, and finding them tearful, the face streaked. And he was torn, because she didn't understand why he had to leave, but he did have to, and it was because of the larger frame of his life and not because of her at all. The ferry was waiting and they'd had a meal together and done all the things you do when someone leaves. And she'd got angry with him and hurled abuse at him, saying he had used her and only wanted her for her tits, and of course it wasn't true, or at least only partly true, and in that moment there had been a pain and sorrow in their hearts that wasn't there before. And there was another couple next to them, a lumpish, English-looking girl with a brilliant blonde crop and an older Greek guy, and she too had quite nice tits starting out from under her shirt, he was always one to notice tits, even in a moment like this, and they were delivering passionate kisses to one another and whispering endearments. And they were going through the same process, he knew, because the girl's eyes were red and the man looked pale and shocked.

So he hugged her and kissed her and felt again the delicate limbs and gentleness of her, but in the end he turned, got on his motorbike, and entered the dark bowels of the ferry. Later, climbing to the upper deck, he stood next to the English girl and looked down on the quay, and there was Dorothea, people milling around her, the Greek guy next to her, yet alone, looking, seeing him. They waved at each other. And how wonderful to be seen off, one of the great privileges of life, that someone cares enough to want to do that.

And they just stood there, him and the English girl, he all the time aware of her tits poking out, and of Dorothea's too, which were actually much better, waving, smiling, passing a shouted word, till the ropes were released and with a boiling of the water, the ferry edged it's way out into the bay. And as it turned she was still there, and minutes later, too, as it went behind the headland and she was out of sight. And they continued to stand for a few moments, still looking behind, he and the English girl, but neither said anything to the other, even though they were probably feeling much the same thing.

He went below then, to find Heine, who had gone to get drinks, leaving the English girl staring at the wake of the ship. Her breasts still poked temptingly out, yet because she was stocky and not like an insect, not attractive to him.

Jurg discovered Heine already into his second beer. He sat down, picked up a can, opened it mechanically and drank. Neither spoke. A fly buzzed round his head but he ignored it.

He noticed that on the wall above Heine's head was an old sepia print. There was a title on a plaque attached to the frame. It said 'Watteau: Pilgrimage to the Island of Love' and the letters were embossed in gold. It showed a group of eighteenth century people with cupids floating over their heads, and they were standing in pairs, each with their different lovers. They were on a Greek island and on one side were the masts of a ship and on the other a statue of Aphrodite. At first it meant nothing to him. But suddenly, he understood what the artist was getting at. It was about how there comes a moment when you have to leave the island of love, and it doesn't matter how you resist it, the moment still comes in the end - there you are on the quay and it's your turn to leave. But he had faith, too, that he would visit it again, as most of us hope to, one day.